Making Room at the Inn

by

Misty Simon

Making Room at the Inn

Cover Art by *Debbie Taylor*

The Wild Rose Press, Inc.
PO Box 708
Adams Basin, NY 14410-0708
Visit us at www.thewildrosepress.com

Publishing History
First Champagne Rose Edition, 2013
Print ISBN 978-1-62830-060-4
Digital ISBN 978-1-62830-061-1

Published in the United States of America

"Is there anything I should know about your life now that's different from before?"

"Like what?"

"Do you like broccoli now? Did you end up finishing college? Do you sleep in the nude?"

She leaned forward in her seat to swat him for that last one. "I don't think you need to know about my sleeping habits. Let's see. We could have fallen in love by email and talking on the phone. Since we've known each other forever, it's not a sudden thing so much as just seeing each other in a different light."

"True."

"So we're getting married because we know we want to be together forever, but we're going to have a long engagement and continue to get to know each other as full-fledged adults instead of all those days together as kids."

"Sounds good to me."

"I'm still going home after the wedding to tie things up, but I'm going to be coming back after I quit my job, to find something up here."

"Okay."

"Aren't you going to help at all?" She blew a breath out, ruffling her bangs.

"Sorry," he said with a smile. "I think you should change the part about finding something up here, though. Don't you think most people will assume you're going to help me with the inn? Plus, jobs of your caliber are in short supply in this area."

"I hadn't thought about that."

"See, I helped."

She swatted him again, and this time he caught her hand.

Dedication

To Daniel,
who is my sprinkles

Chapter One

For what felt like the millionth time, Chelsea Moore belted out a popular kids' song with her four-year-old daughter singing along in the back seat. She loved her daughter, she did, but even she had her limits on the number of times she could sing the same song without pulling out her hair.

Thankfully, the inn where they'd be staying for the next eight days was around only one more bend. It couldn't come soon enough, as far as she was concerned. Though Chelsea was willing to do nearly anything to make her baby girl happy, she had thought Mazzy would at least take a nap during the three-hour car ride. No such luck.

The late summer sun warmed the earth and brought the smell of home to her nose. No matter how long she'd been gone, there was no mistaking the fertile earth of central Pennsylvania in August.

As she had been instructed in her final email exchange with the owner of the Barton Inn, she pulled her car around back. Once she parked, she popped the locks on the car and hustled around to release her wiggly daughter from her booster seat. Mazzy had been an angel for the last three hours, but she would definitely need some run-around time.

"We're here!" Mazzy yelled, and went straight for the grass, to run and jump and twirl.

"We're here," Chelsea echoed as she turned to survey the packed-to-the-brim back seat. With her hands on her hips, she shook her head. She didn't even want to think about the trunk, full of all the things they would need over the next week.

The desire to get down in the grass with her daughter and play nearly overwhelmed her. But there were things to do, and no one else was going to do them. She'd been alone for almost two years and had gotten used to doing for herself.

"Come on, Pumpkin. We need to get our stuff inside. Then we can play."

Mazzy came running at top speed and stopped at the side of the car with a beaming smile. Chelsea's heart melted, as it always did with the sight of that smile. There were so many things that had gone wrong over the last several years, but Mazzy made it all worth it.

"I want to carry stuff, Mommy. Let me help!" She stood with her arms straight out in front of her, the eager beaver.

Chelsea gave her a light grocery bag filled with stuffed animals and sent her on her way. Of course, Mazzy didn't make it all the way to the door, stopping at the flowers bordering the wide veranda to chase a butterfly back and forth along the railing. Turning toward the filled back seat, Chelsea sighed. Her daughter would be fine for a couple of minutes. They were out in the country, after all, in a small valley that made it seem as if they were the only ones around for miles.

The trip had been long, and it was going to take time to get everything she'd brought into this palatial home. She would take it one step at a time until she knew what kind of space she was working with. She'd become methodical since her husband had become an ex-husband. One foot in front of the other was the only way she had made it through.

Her sister, Belinda, was finally getting married to the man she'd been with for years. The original wedding planner, Paige, was one of Chelsea's best friends from growing up and had been booked a year in advance. But then she had been put on bed rest for the last ten weeks due to her difficult pregnancy. Chelsea hadn't hesitated when Paige called to ask if she could take over the job. Chelsea's only other duty during this week of vacation was being maid of honor, so she would be fine. Especially since everything was already very neatly and precisely laid out for the wedding of her sister's dreams.

Grabbing the nearest suitcase, Chelsea also hefted her laptop bag onto her shoulder. She bumped the back door of the car closed with her hip, then took a step toward the house and ran into a solid wall that had not been there before.

Strong hands gripped the bare flesh of her upper arms and made warmth spread from her hairline to her toes. She looked up—and up—into the deep blue eyes of her best friend's brother. "If it isn't Jack Barton."

"Then who is it?" he asked in a voice that was a lot lower than it had been all those years ago.

Of course it was lower, she chided herself while she laughed. He was twenty-seven to her twenty-five. Did she expect his voice to still crack every once in a while?

"Aren't you a sight for sore eyes?" He held her out

at arms' length, and she fought the urge to squirm under his perusal. "You look good, Chelsea."

She was as short as she'd ever been, though curvier than she was in high school. The fluttering in her stomach was unusual and unwarranted, but she smiled, anyway. His stare made her very aware of his skin touching hers, so she bumped up the wattage on her smile, putting the feeling down to nerves rattling around in her stomach from the many things she needed to do over the next eight days.

"You look good, too. I can't believe it's been so long since I've been here. Have you changed much?"

He laughed, the sound rumbling along her skin. "Yeah, I'd say I've changed quite a bit since I last saw you."

The pause while her head caught up with his joke was a little embarrassing. "Oh, you're too funny." And with his corny joke breaking the tension, she was back on regular footing. "I meant to the inn. Have you changed things here?"

"To some extent, but the rooms have stayed relatively the same. I put you in the Pembroke Room. Paige reminded me it was always your favorite. Why don't you hand me your stuff, and we'll get you settled?" He took the suitcase from her, then looped the strap of her laptop case over his broad shoulder. What had seemed so overwhelming when she held it all looked like nearly nothing in his big hands.

"Let me grab a few things, and I'll follow you in."

"Why don't you load me up first? I can carry quite a bit more than this."

So she piled him high with bags, looping them around his thick wrist and ignoring the way the glancing touches of his fingers felt like so much more than they really were—accidental brushes that meant nothing.

What on earth was wrong with her? Maybe it was the country air.

She pulled more bags from the back seat, amazed she had managed to stow all this in her compact car and hopeful she hadn't forgotten anything. Of course, if she had forgotten something, she could always prevail on her mother. She didn't want to start her first vacation home in many years with requests for help, though. There was a rift here with her family she wanted to mend. In her quest to keep her life in Bettleton as smooth as possible, she'd not had a ton of interaction with her family. She hoped to change that with this visit.

Once she was as loaded down as Jack, she called for Mazzy and began the walk up to the place they would call home for just a little while.

****

Chelsea Moore was back in his house and would be for the next week and a day. It was good to see her and see her happy. The last time they had been together she'd had a smile on her lips but sadness in her eyes. But this was a different Chelsea, one who had aged in the best possible way. He couldn't help but notice that her dips and curves had only been enhanced in the years since he had seen her last. Though he shouldn't be noticing that at all, because she was one of his sister's best friends and therefore had always been off limits.

"Let's put everything down in the drawing room. Then we'll figure out where you want it all. We have plenty of time, so there's no rush. I've made sure you'll have the whole inn to yourself this week. We had other people try to book, but your sister very explicitly informed me that this week was about her and that included keeping the inn clear of everyone but you. She and Marcus will be here for their first night as a married couple, but until then you have the run of the place."

Her gaze tracked beyond him. "Well, me and the munchkin."

"Right, the munchkin." He hadn't forgotten she had a child; it just had slipped his mind for a moment while he took in all the changes from the very young Chelsea he'd known to this new Chelsea. Her previously long, light brown hair now ended at her shoulders in some sort of swingy hairdo, framing her full cheeks and setting off eyes the color of amber.

"Mazzy, come here," she said for the second time, waving to where a little girl was walking through the bed of flowers near the deck railing. He bit back a groan. Hopefully she hadn't ruined the landscaping. What he knew about plant placement and growth could fit on the back of a bar napkin, and he didn't want to have to bring the gardener back just yet.

Mazzy came running at full tilt at them. The way her cinnamon-colored braids flew in the air took him back to a place twenty years ago when Chelsea had looked just like this, with the same slightly upturned nose and round face. She and his sister, Paige, had been inseparable, and so he had also grown up with her, even though they had bugged the hell out of him when they were little.

"Wow, she looks just like you."

"No," the little girl said with her hands on her hips, coming to an abrupt halt in front of him. "My mommy looks just like me." She gave him a toothy grin before skipping around her mom fast enough to make him dizzy.

"She has a lot of energy and a lot of sass." Chelsea used the palm of her hand to brush the top of Mazzy's hair as she skipped by again.

"Sounds like someone I used to know."

She laughed, a sound he hadn't heard in ages. An LOL over email during the course of the last four weeks was nothing like hearing her infectious bell-tone laugh. "I still have the sass. But the energy? Not so much."

Those amber eyes sparkled up at him and were joined by a second pair a heartbeat later. Mazzy stood on the front of her mother's sneakers with her arms wrapped around Chelsea's waist, swinging back and forth with her face tipped to the midmorning sky.

"I don't believe that for a moment." He took her in from head to toe, admiring the way she filled out the shirt and jeans that gripped her every hill and valley. He tried not to be too obvious. There was, after all, a child standing between them. And the fact that Chelsea had always been off limits. He must remember that last part. "Let's get inside and set you up." He walked past the two of them with his hands full and cleared his throat when Mazzy started singing in a voice exactly like one he had heard many times when playing games and running through the woods behind his house.

Throwing the side door open, he waited for the two beauties to precede him into the house where he and Paige had grown up and where he now made his living.

It was strange to see Chelsea back here. The two girls had often run roughshod over the place in elementary school, then hung out in various rooms during high school. It wasn't often he was far away, since his parents had the inn to run and asked him to keep his eye on the two of them.

When she'd emailed him four weeks ago to say she was taking over the wedding planning for Paige, he'd been enthusiastic to see her again, figuring they'd pick up where they left off with their friendship, like having an old buddy stop in for the weekend. But those curves were shattering that notion, and so was her smile and laugh.

They hadn't spoken in years, until his sister had given Chelsea his email address and they'd exchanged information online to keep track of things. A phone call might have been easier, but he preferred a paper trail he could go back to. And now he was almost happy he had gone the email route, because the voice was lower, the cadence sexier, in a way that might just have had him dreaming over the last few weeks. Her body lived up to the promise of that husky voice in ways he would never have dreamed when they were teenagers.

And Paige would have his head if she had any inkling of where his poor brain was wandering. She'd warned him away from her best friend when he was seventeen, and he had a feeling the sentiment wouldn't be any different now.

Well, he'd just have to figure out some way to squash those thoughts, or this was going to be a long week.

****

"Come in, and welcome," a short, plump redhead said with enthusiasm as she hovered in the hallway. Her gusto was so out there, Chelsea couldn't help but smile. "I'm Adele, and I'm here to help."

"I'm Chelsea. And I'd shake your hand, but I'm afraid I'll drop something."

"I'm Mazzy, and you can shake my hand!"

With a nod, Adele shook Mazzy's hand, then turned to Chelsea. "Let me take something, and I'll show you into the drawing room. We'll get you set up in no time at all."

"I'm actually perfectly balanced right now," Chelsea answered, laughing. "If you take anything, I'm afraid I'll drop it all. But if you wouldn't mind leading the way, that would be great."

"As long as you're sure." Adele didn't look sure, but she walked farther into the house without protesting again.

Chelsea had brief glimpses of the sitting room and highly polished floors as she made her way down the hall behind Adele, Mazzy skipping between and around them. The door to the drawing room was to the right, and Chelsea couldn't be happier to set down her load. Jack followed close behind with more of her things. There was so much space in this room, her entire kitchen, living room, and dining room would have easily fit into it.

"You can take over this whole room," Jack said, entering behind them. "I don't plan on having anything in here during this week other than you. We have a more informal parlor across the hallway that I thought we'd use for the get-togethers Paige arranged for everyone before the wedding."

Yes, it was all in the stack of folders and notebooks she spied lined up with military precision on a shelf to the right of the spacious desk. She was going to be spending a lot of time with those notebooks. And probably on the phone with Paige.

"That'll be great. I think Belinda will like it in there. Plus, it'll give me a chance to get everything up and running. Are you sure you don't want me to just use my bedroom, instead? I remember the room you're giving me, and it's huge. What about just putting a desk in and letting me hole up there? I hate to take up this entire room with my stuff."

One of his dark eyebrows shot up and the right side of his mouth quirked. "I could have sworn I remembered you begging to be allowed to hang in this room when you were younger. I thought I'd give it to you now. And I already have the whole thing set up to the letter of Paige Law."

"Thanks, then. I guess I should just graciously accept it and keep my mouth shut."

"Sounds like a good plan." His wide smile was so cheesy she nearly punched him in the arm like old times.

"Don't you think you should be nicer to our guest, Boss?" Adele asked.

"Nah, we've known each other too long to deal with the niceties." The look in his eyes was a teasing one she had forgotten—or had made herself forget when it would have been so easy to go back to the past in her mind, where things were easier.

"That's true." Chelsea scoped out the room. As she turned in a full circle, she took in everything Paige had dragooned Jack into setting up. It was stacked with boxes Chelsea knew were filled with fabrics and all the things Belinda had been collecting over the last year. Once she took everything out and started sorting to her preference, the space would probably be crowded no matter how big it was. "So, speaking of no niceties, why don't you go haul your rear end out to my car and bring in the rest of the stuff, like a good boy?"

Adele snorted, then quickly covered her mouth with her hand.

"I'll get you for that later." Jack squeezed Chelsea's shoulder as he walked by her. She caught a hint of man and cologne and she locked the knees that wanted to turn to jelly at the smell of him.

"Yeah, well, you can get me after you get all my luggage." She laughed as she said it, but couldn't help checking out the view as he walked away. He was one mighty fine specimen of man. His dark hair curled just at the edge of his polo shirt's collar, while his broad shoulder stretched the fabric to perfection. The fit of his jeans was nothing to sneeze at, either. And he was her best friend's brother, always off limits. In fact, she'd never even thought of him that way until just now. It really must be the country air.

"Why don't I show you to your room upstairs while we let him bring in your things?" Adele stepped back from the window seat with a smile. "By the way, I think I'm going to like you."

"I already know I like you." It was nice to be welcomed and to feel the sentiment was real. Except for her job and her time with Mazzy, that feeling had been in short supply lately.

"Then we'll get along just fine," Adele said, leading the way up the stairs.

As Chelsea trailed her hand along the satiny smooth finish of the banister, Mazzy ran up and down the stairs behind and in front of her. Better the girl get all that energy out now rather than tonight when it was time for bed. After the long car ride and all the packing, Chelsea herself was ready for a nap. But then she would never sleep tonight. Despite her teasing that Jack should bring in everything for her, she really only wanted to see her room for a moment, and then she'd go down to help.

It was as breathtaking as she remembered. A queen-sized four-poster bed was set off to one side, massive but not dominating in the enormous room. A dresser and vanity in the same dark wood accompanied it. Along the left wall was the sitting area, which boasted a couch and two chairs in burgundy. The door on the far wall led to a smaller bedroom with a twin bed and its own dresser.

This was going to be heaven.

"I hope everything will be okay," Adele said from the doorway, hovering again, hands clasped at her waist.

"Oh my, yes. I might not ever want to move out." Chelsea skimmed a hand over the purple, green, and blue brocade coverlet on the bed.

"You aren't the first person to say that." Adele brushed at her bangs. "Anyway, everything you could possibly need is in the bathroom to your right. If you find something we haven't provided, all you have to do is ask. I'm here on the property this whole week. I hope you enjoy your stay."

"I have a feeling that's not going to be a problem at all." Other than that blip downstairs when her friend from a lifetime ago had turned into something a little more dangerous for a moment, she would be just fine. Once this vacation was over and her sister was happily married, she would go back home to grab with both hands the promotion she had been promised at work. Hopefully then things would get better, and she and Mazzy could move forward with their lives instead of simply existing.

Mazzy jumped on the bed in the next room, the springs creaking. Chelsea hustled to the door, peeked her head into the room, and told her, "No. We've still got the same rules as home, bubby. No jumping on the bed, and make sure you're on your best behavior when we're here. You can do it." She rubbed a hand over her daughter's soft, braided hair and turned to go back into her own room, only to find Jack standing in her doorway with his arms and ankles crossed and a smile on his handsome face.

"If I remember correctly, there was someone else who always bounced on beds when she was younger."

"Don't say that too loud or you're going to ruin my authority." She pulled the door closed to Mazzy's room, keeping it from shutting all the way but giving them some privacy.

"She's a great kid." He stayed right where he was, lounging against the door as if he had nothing else to do all day.

She, on the other hand, had a ton of things to do, and more to come once she called her mother and Paige to let them know she was in town. She'd thought about putting it off but was sure it would be all over the place by now.

"Yeah, thanks. I'll get her in a second, and then I have to run out to see Paige. All this wedding planning stuff was not in the plans when I originally booked my vacation. I hope I can handle it all."

"You will. And I'm here to help, too. Adele also

offered to take on some of the duties for you. And I highly doubt Paige will give you a moment's peace no matter how much she's supposed to keep the stress down and her feet up. Here's her key, by the way, so you can get in without having to make her get up out of bed."

With an economy of movement that sent her pulse stumbling, he unfolded his burly body from the door and took a step into the room. Suddenly the spacious room felt a whole lot smaller. He handed her the key. Her fingers brushed his palm as she took the piece of metal, warm from his touch, and something surprisingly like a burst of want ferreted up her spine. Want had been in short supply in her life for the last few years, too, and now was not the time for it to reappear. Needs like providing a home for Mazzy and working to make sure she had everything necessary, those she understood. Want she could do without.

Though her brain felt a little short-circuited, she didn't miss the way Mazzy continued to jump on the bed, just with smaller bounces.

"Mackenzie Jane, no jumping."

"Okay." The disappointment was clear in the little girl's voice, but it couldn't be helped. Eventually they would go back to their home. Chelsea did not want to fight to undo the bad habits that could be formed in a week of play time.

Jack leaned closer and dropped his voice. "She really is fine. That bed has seen a ton of children who have jumped, leaped, bounced, and flounced on it."

"I'm sure that's true, but we have rules and she knows them."

He flicked the end of her hair and smiled at her. "I

like her name, but I like Mazzy better. Where'd you get it?"

"Well, when she was little, she had trouble saying her whole name, so she started calling herself Mazzy and then Belinda called her Snazzy Mazzy, which she loved. I guess it stuck."

"I like it."

It was difficult not to breathe him in again as his voice ran over and through her mind. The sound alone created a haze of something she did not want to examine right now, especially when combined with the purely masculine smell of him. This was a boy from long ago and a man who she had only recently reconnected with because of her sister's wedding and Paige's doctor-enforced bed rest. They had nothing in common anymore except some old memories and a desire to have this wedding go off without a hitch. She would do well to remember that.

Making deliberate contact with those blue eyes again, she focused all her energy on making sure not to look down and take in the way his body had filled out in all the right places. He had been a late bloomer but had definitely grown up while she was gone.

"I do mean that, Chelsea," he said, his voice low and soft, like warm honey pouring over her. "Anything you need while you're here, you just have to ask. Nothing is too big or too small. Adele and I want this to be the best possible wedding."

"Adele and you?" She couldn't resist teasing him even as she was desperately trying to recover from the feel of his voice through her veins.

"Strictly business," he said.

"Not even a dalliance?"

"When have you known me to dally?" He smiled, but there was something in his eyes she couldn't read.

"Wait, I remember that one girl—Sally? Tally? Tabby! Tabby, in tenth grade, with the humungous mane of black hair and the boobs out to here." She cupped her hands in front of her own chest much farther out than was anatomically and naturally possible, especially for a sixteen-year-old.

"What are you doing, Mommy? Are you playing a game? Is that the one with Ms. Mary Mack all dressed in black? I want to play!" Mazzy came running into the room and jumped onto the bigger mattress, swinging on the posts of the bed.

Chelsea grasped her daughter's wrist gently but firmly and brought her to a standstill. "I said no jumping, and I meant it. Remember, best behavior." She said it as quietly and discreetly as she could.

"So will you be ready for a high tea once you get back from seeing Aunt Paige?" Jack asked in the silence after Chelsea's reprimand but before Mazzy's bottom lip fully came out.

"High tea?" Mazzy said, all trace of any tears or quivering bottom lip gone. "What's a high tea?"

She had scrambled off the bed and came to stand in front of him. Jack must have felt like he was towering over her small form, because he hunkered down to her level, his back to Chelsea. "It's where we go talk the cook into making up fancy tea and giving us cookies before dinner. What do you think?"

He glanced over his shoulder at Chelsea and she gave him a nod and a smile. A smile that was echoed but with fewer teeth on the little girl in front of him.

She would have to make sure Mazzy did not end

up attached to this man or this place. It was too easy to imagine hanging out here all the time. Having her family nearby to help and to nurture. To make it so Chelsea didn't have to go it alone.

But that was a fantasy. She had made her bed and now she had to lie in it. Mazzy wasn't suffering from living with a single parent. She wasn't suffering from having no other blood family close by. Chelsea didn't want to move her away from her dad, just in case he started taking an interest in her. And these vacations could become more frequent once she got the promotion at work and the funds that went with the promotion. She just had to get through the next week, and then she'd be golden.

Keeping that thought in the forefront of her mind, she took Mazzy's hand. There was no good reason why they couldn't enjoy everything offered here in the meantime, though.

"We'd love to have high tea. We'll be back in about two hours, and then we can beautify ourselves and be down."

"I'll wait for you," he said, with an overdone bow at the waist. He winked at Mazzy as he pulled the door shut with a soft click.

"I like the big man," Mazzy said as she trotted to her room.

Chelsea did, too, and hoped that wasn't going to be a problem. She missed home far more than she had thought possible.

A few minutes later a knock sounded on the door, breaking Chelsea out of her thoughts. She glanced at the clock to make sure she hadn't lost track of time.

Jack was standing in the hallway when she opened

the door, his arms full of bright colors and plastic.

"I didn't know if you had anything appropriate for high tea, so I rummaged around upstairs and came up with a few things." He passed the bundle over to her without a problem. She had more trouble as she struggled to keep the slippery plastic from falling to the floor. "See you this afternoon."

Then he was gone, pulling the door closed behind him again.

Staggering over to the bed, she dumped everything on the comforter. She reached into the pile and pulled out a dress obviously meant for a child. After removing the plastic garment bag, she shook out the long electric blue dress with an empire waist trimmed in lace. It even had a small purse in the same color. It would be a little big for Mazzy, but she would love it as much as Chelsea had loved dressing up in it many years ago.

Something velvety and dark purple caught her eye in the rest of the pile. She dug through, coming up with another plastic bag. The dress would hit the floor on her and also had an empire waist, but that was where the similarities ended. This one had a chiffon overlay for the skirt that appeared iridescent, with long ribbons of the same filmy material wrapped around the bodice.

Just short of tearing open the bag, she pulled out the dress as fast as she could, then laid it on the bed to get a better view. Small stars made of clusters of crystals dotted the neckline. The dress was sleeveless and honestly one of the most divine things she had ever seen. She remembered Jack and Paige's mom going out for a night at the theater in it once, when Chelsea and Paige were about ten, and she had drooled over it then. She'd try it on right after she'd been to see Paige and made sure her friend was as okay as she'd sounded over the phone during their many conversations.

Her cell phone rang as she was hanging the dresses up in the closet. Great, her mom. She adored her mother, but the woman was on a rampage lately and was almost worse than the bride with her demands.

"Hey, Mom. I was just going to call you."

"Of course you were. Now, we have a lot to go over once you get back from seeing Paige, and I want to make sure you have time to get settled in, but I am going to need to see that granddaughter of mine as soon as possible."

"We'll see you first thing tomorrow for the dress fittings. I just want to get unpacked and make sure I have everything from Paige, and then we're yours for the next week." Chelsea turned away from Mazzy so the little girl couldn't see her roll her eyes.

"That's the plan. I'm so happy you're here!"

"And I'm happy to be here. But I really should go so we can get over to Paige's. I have some things that I hope will make her convalescence easier."

"She'll love that. Make sure you got her some trashy magazines."

Chelsea laughed. "I did. Now I'd better get going. Do you want to say hi to Mazzy real quick while I hang a few things up?"

"Of course, hon, and I hope you brought some of your nice clothes, because I have a few men I'd like you to meet this week."

"Mom!"

"Don't you 'mom' me. They're perfectly nice men I won't set you up on any blind dates, I promise. These will just be informal meet-ups where I casually mention that you're available. Actually, I've already mentioned that, but now they'll get to see how pretty you are, instead of just the pictures on my mantel."

Oh, God. It was going to be a freaking bachelor parade. "I don't want to meet any...one." She was careful not to mention the word men, since it might lead to questions from Mazzy.

"Of course you do. And it wouldn't hurt if they lived out here, since maybe then you would finally move back home. Now, it's just one or two men, maybe four. I can't remember, but it won't be painful. Just dress nice."

"I have to go. We'll see you tomorrow." And she hung up because there was no arguing with her mother. Leigh Moore didn't understand why Chelsea stayed in Bettleton. Chelsea hadn't tried to explain, only saying that she had her job and they had a life there. In reality, though, she hoped one day Mazzy's father would wake up and realize he had a daughter who needed him. Chelsea didn't want him back for herself, but she wasn't going to move away, just in case he came to understand that Mazzy should have him in her life. He wouldn't ever do that if they lived three hours away. They were already out of mind. She didn't want to also be out of sight.

She loathed putting Mazzy back in the car after so many hours on the road, but it couldn't be helped. And her little munchkin was fine with it, asking for the same song they'd been singing before, and bouncing along in her booster seat.

The drive was no more than twenty minutes, but it felt like a whole different world. Where Jack's town of Kissinger was small and quaint, with buildings from the

1800s and privately owned storefronts, Paige lived in the city. It felt like being back in her new hometown.

She navigated the one-way streets and heavy traffic with years of experience she hadn't had when she first started driving. Her parents had made her drive in the city so she wouldn't be afraid to do it later, but the past eight years of living in Bettleton had refined her deftness. Pulling up in front of Paige's townhouse, she parallel parked like a pro, then waited for the stoplight behind her to turn red so she could safely get out and run around to Mazzy's side of the car.

Mazzy held her hand while she reached into the backseat for the few things she'd brought for Paige. She needed comfort stuff, especially since she would be shut up in her apartment for the next six weeks on absolute bed rest until it was time for the baby to come.

Letting herself into the townhouse, Chelsea called out a greeting.

"I'm back here, lounging like the whale I am!" Paige yelled from down the hall. "I'd come greet you, but Baby Sarian is not having any of it today."

Chelsea had not visited since Paige had bought herself this townhouse, so she did her best to navigate through the warren of rooms to find where "back here" was.

Pictures hung on the wall—the two of them in pigtails and huge smiles. Black and whites that Paige must have had made after the fact, since they had used only color film in their cameras back in the day. One color one sat in the middle of the arrangement with the two of them hanging out either side of the tiny tree house Jack had built them when they were ten to his almost thirteen.

She hurried down the hall to avoid thinking too much about Jack.

"Here we are!" Mazzy said, bouncing into the room filled with glass vases in a multitude of colors, each vase holding a candle glowing softly. Chelsea had thought perhaps Mazzy had gotten all her energy out with the running up and down the stairs, but apparently that was not true. Thank goodness she had brought along some coloring books for her so they didn't disrupt the tranquility that Paige had made out of her townhouse.

"Come give Auntie Paige a kiss, monkey."

Mazzy giggled and made monkey sounds while she climbed up onto the bed next to Paige.

"Are you sure she should be up there? Don't you need to rest?"

"God! I'm up to my eyebrows in rest. She's not going to do anything to me, and it's not like I'm fragile, just on rest detail to make sure Sarian stays where he or she is supposed to for a little bit longer."

Chelsea started taking things out of her tote and placing them on the bench at the foot of Paige's bed. She had coloring books, crayons, a picture book for Mazzy, and her favorite teddy, along with her blanket in case she got tired. Chelsea didn't plan on staying longer than an hour, but naps could happen spontaneously with Mazzy, and she wanted to be prepared.

"Are you really going to name the baby Sarian?" She tripped over her next words in case she'd offended the potentially emotional Paige. "Not that it's not a perfectly good name. I just haven't heard it before."

Paige laughed. "No, it's a combo of Sara and Ian.

I'm not going to find out the se-, gender of the baby until they show him or her to me after labor, but those are the two names I've picked out for him or her. I combined them when I went on bed rest to make sure I have something to call the baby when I spend countless hours telling him or her to behave and how much I love him or her. See? Him or her over and over again gets old. So the name gives me a way to connect without knowing what's coming."

"Makes perfect sense."

"I knew you'd understand."

"Of course."

"I understand too, Auntie Paige! Can I see Sarian?"

"Oh, honey, Sarian is still in the belly for a little while longer, but you can rub the baby's head if you want. It's right here, sitting on my bladder."

Paige took Mazzy's hand and guided her in a series of small circles. Chelsea smiled, remembering rubbing Mazzy in the same way and wishing she would get out from under her ribs.

"So what's new?" Chelsea sat on the other side of the bed and rubbed what was most likely Sarian's rear end.

"Nothing at all. I have a woman who's coming in twice a week to clean, and my mom keeps threatening to come home from her trip to take care of me. But so far I've held her off. I love her, but I don't think I could handle her living in my house, no matter what."

"I wish I could take the time off to stay with you."

"Now we both know that's not possible. You have your big promotion coming up, and a life over in Bettleton. I have plenty of people stopping in with meals and groceries and smiles to keep me company.

Plus, Jack comes by at least every other day."

The mention of Jack sent that same frisson of want up Chelsea's spine, but she tamped it down ruthlessly. "That's nice of him."

"It is. Then again, he's always been the nice one in the family." Her cheeky smile made Chelsea smile, too. "How are you doing at the inn? All set up?"

"We're doing fine, and, no, not yet. We just got here about an hour ago." Her own marriage had taken place at the justice of the peace and had fallen apart shortly thereafter, but that didn't mean she couldn't pull this off. Paige had armed her with a ton of lists that would guide her.

"So Jack hasn't shown you all the things I ordered him to have ready for you? I think the man had to come over with the house van twice."

"Oh, lord, now you're making me nervous. I don't know if I'm going to be able to do your job like you."

"It'll be fine. You have everything you need plus some extra, and Jack's done this before, so you won't be alone. I'm only a phone call away, too. I can't believe I won't be there, though. I've been looking forward to this for a year!"

"I wish you were going, too, but you have to look out for Sarian."

"I know, I know. But for being such an active person, this is killing me." She harrumphed and scooched down in the bed. She looked like Mazzy had, with her bottom lip almost trembling, right before Jack invited them to high tea. Chelsea did not need to be thinking about Jack when she was sitting on the edge of his sister's bed. Paige would kill them both if they started anything at all. He was the big brother, not hot guy material. She absolutely had to remember that.

"Is there anything I can do while I'm here? Clean your kitchen? Bathroom? Something? Actually, let me make you lunch, and then you can tell me what else to do to feel useful."

Mazzy continued talking with Paige, and Chelsea smiled every time she heard the two of them laugh. She came back bearing a tray with a fruit salad, juice, and some sort of chicken casserole. "We're going to have a picnic."

She spread out a tablecloth on top of Paige's bedspread, mindful of Mazzy's tendency to spill. But everything was eaten without a hitch, and she washed the dishes, then came back to ask what else needed to be done.

"You can sit with me and tell me all about what's been going on with you. I want to catch up. Email and the phone just aren't the same as having you face to face."

Chelsea should have come to visit more before this. Five years was too long to be away from her friend.

"Before you start feeling all terrible about some imagined thing, don't. We've both had our own lives, and I've come over to visit you many times. I just miss you. I'm not blaming you."

Biting her lip, Chelsea nodded her head. "I still feel bad."

"And I'll get up and kick your a-, rear end if you don't stop right now. It's the way of life. No need to apologize. We're busy. You've got Mazzy. I have a business that runs every weekend when you are available. It happens. Plus, I'm sure I'll be burning up your phone line when this baby comes, since I have no idea what I'm doing."

"You're going to be a wonderful mother."

"Yeah, I just wish I had chosen a better father," Paige said, then clamped her lips tight and darted a glance at Mazzy.

"Hey, bubby, let's set up in the next room with your coloring book so you can make Auntie Paige some pictures for her walls."

"Yay!"

Chelsea took a few moments to get her daughter situated, kissed her on the head, then went back to Paige's room.

"I'm sorry about that," her friend said as soon as Chelsea stepped over the threshold.

"No, don't be sorry. Though I have to say that at least you know he's a bastard before the big event. Maybe it will be easier for you."

"Aw, honey, who would have ever thought we'd be in these predicaments, huh? I didn't exactly foresee this with the Chinese fortunetellers we used when we were younger."

That made Chelsea laugh. They'd consulted those things for finding out everything from who they'd marry to what kind of job they'd have and what car they'd drive. "No, of course not. I just wish it would have worked out better for you."

"Yeah, well, at least I don't have to have the experience of the perfect pregnancy husband and then find out the father/husband doesn't live up to the fantasy. It's going to be fine. I have a lot of support in the area."

Something Chelsea did not have back in Bettleton. But this visit wasn't about her.

"Are you sure there's nothing I can do while I'm here? I even brought cleaning gloves with me, if you need something done."

"No, just hang out with me for a while."

"Okay, but first let me show you the goodies I brought." She dug back into the tote and came up with a whole series of romance novels and a stack of trashy tabloid magazines that Paige had been saying she wanted to read if she ever had time.

"Oh, these are perfect! Now I can see who's with whom and dream about finding that perfect ending. You're the best, Chelsea!"

"I brought you one of those triangle peg games, too, to test your smarts. Maybe you can master it now."

"That's going to be tortuous, but if I can finally have only one peg left on the triangle like you've had, then it might just be worth it."

"I could show you how it's done."

"No, no! Don't ruin the fun!"

They laughed, and Chelsea enjoyed the way the sound was no different from when they were teenagers. She reached across and hugged Paige, whispering, "I have missed you, and if you need anything at all, you know you just have to call. It's not an easy road you're taking. I know."

They separated, and Chelsea was surprised to see tears in her happy-go-lucky friend's eyes.

"It's not one I chose, it's the one I've been plopped on. But I have you to look up to. You've made it, and so can I."

That took Chelsea aback. She didn't think she had made anything. She'd felt more like she'd been stumbling in a circle. "I…"

"Don't even say it. I'm on the outside looking in, and from here you have a wonderfully happy child, one who thinks you're the greatest. Can you really ask for more?"

"No, I guess not. But being here in town is making me realize how little help I have, and how few friends."

"Ha! How could you ever find someone as awesome as me?"

They laughed.

Then Chelsea abruptly stopped. "Mazzy is going to start asking questions soon, when she goes to preschool and realizes other kids have fathers in their lives on a more permanent basis. I'm not looking forward to that. Right now she assumes everyone lives with their mom and has a father somewhere who they don't see often. I know I should talk to her, but I just can't yet. She doesn't ask about him. Do you think she should?"

"Probably not yet. And I know you keep hoping he'll get a clue before you have to tell her that he's not interested in anything more than the creation."

"Yeah, I'm not going to say it's the smartest thing I've ever done, but I just can't seem to leave when I have hope that he'll be there for her once school starts and there are concerts to go to, and award ceremonies, and dance recitals. I bet he'll come to that kind of thing."

"Oh, honey, I'm not sure what to tell you. You'll deal with it when it comes, though, and then I can learn that from you, too."

They laughed again, and Chelsea shoved that worry down to much farther along on her worries list. If Mazzy wasn't asking, then Chelsea wasn't going to worry about it yet. The answer would come to her when the time was right. Either that, or her waiting around would have paid off.

They talked about inconsequential things until Paige seemed to tire. "I think I'm going to nap."

Chelsea took a peek at her watch and realized it had been well over an hour. "I'm here this whole week, and you've got me so organized, I'll be able to spare time if you want me here."

"No, you do the wedding thing, because that's what I want you to do. Call me. We'll chat and laugh. I'll feel better knowing you're no more than twenty minutes away instead of hours."

Mazzy came in with a handful of drawings she spread out all over Paige's bed. Paige oohed and ahhed over every single one, and then they took their leave.

"We'll be back."

"And I'll be fine. Watch out for that brother of mine this week, though. Don't let him big-brother you like he used to!"

"No worries. I probably won't have much interaction with him since I'll be so busy and he will too."

They said their goodbyes and Chelsea got Mazzy back in her car seat. She'd had a great time with Paige and wished she had taken the time to make these kinds of friendships back in Bettleton instead of always concentrating so much time on Paul. She couldn't go back, though, so she made up her mind to make more of an effort once this week was over.

The drive back to the inn was filled with Mazzy chattering on about Sarian and maybe Chelsea could have another baby some day because Mazzy would like to pet them and love them.

Chelsea didn't explain anything, just let her babble on. As far as she was concerned, Mazzy was it, and that was okay with her. She wouldn't suffer for being an only child. Even if she could get Paul to finally pay attention to their daughter, she had no intention of ever getting back together with him, nor did she want to date anyone. Unbidden, an image of Jack popped into her head, and she shut it right down. Not going there.

Back at the inn after the twenty-minute drive, she was surprised to find Mazzy still wide awake. She had been so quiet, with her head ducked down since they'd crossed the bridge ten minutes ago, that Chelsea had thought she'd fallen asleep. Instead, the little girl was hard at work, concentrating on coloring. She'd thought for sure she would have fallen asleep. Well, at least she'd sleep well tonight.

They made a beeline for their rooms. After shrugging out of her clothes, Chelsea pulled the burgundy dress from the garment bag and slipped it over her head. The inside was lined with what felt like silk as the cool fabric slid over her body. With the ribbons undone, they trailed along the floor, but once she'd crisscrossed them over her waist, they made a kind of corset. She quick-stepped over to the full-length mirror, where she drew in a sharp breath at the beauty of the dress. It was magnificent. And way too decadent for two o'clock in the afternoon, when she should be getting everything set up and running for the wedding.

"Wow, so pretty!" Mazzy said from behind her. "I want to be so pretty, too."

"Your dress is on the bed, sweet pea. Why don't you bring it to me and we'll try it on?"

The fit was just as Chelsea had expected, a little on

the large side, but Mazzy didn't seem to notice. She loved to dress up in big-girl clothes, so the way the dress hung didn't bother her.

"I should wear my crown."

"Absolutely."

"We should wear makeup, too." Mazzy looked at Chelsea out of the corner of her eye with a sly smile.

Chelsea laughed. She was going to have her hands full when this one was a teenager. "Okay, we'll wear makeup, too."

"Yippie!"

"We're only going to have tea, though, and then we have to come back up to change and get down to work. Auntie Belinda is counting on us."

"I know," Mazzy sing-songed from the other room.

. Mazzy was her happy light. Chelsea didn't want to spoil these moments for her. What could it hurt to spend an hour at high tea? There was no reason she shouldn't have fun while they were here. Chelsea had plenty of time to get everything organized. Paige, bless her heart, had already done most of it for her.

Besides, this was supposed to be her vacation, too.

Chapter Two

"Ladies, thank you for agreeing to meet me and for showing up so promptly." Two hours after his spontaneous invitation, Jack, in a tux with tails, ushered the Moore ladies into the formal parlor with a wide sweep of his arm. "You both look stunning."

Chelsea dropped a curtsy in a flowing gown that had once belonged to his mother. He'd found it tucked up in the attic. Thank God for plastic wrapping and airtight trunks. And for women who weren't afraid to be womanly. Little Mazzy was wearing a dress he vaguely remembered from back in the day, and he thanked Paige's hoarding tactics. A tiara perched on the child's head—she not only looked like a true princess, she carried herself regally, too.

And the little princess thrust a picture at him. "That's a thank you for high tea, Big Man."

Wild with color, it was a picture of a prince standing below a tower waiting for his long-haired beauty to come down from her small window. He'd treasure it.

"Thank you."

"Thank yous can come with kisses, Big Man," the little girl said slyly.

She was a hoot, but he gave her a peck on the forehead and said thank you again.

The table was set with tea steeping in a porcelain

teapot from his mother's collection. He poured out half a cup for Mazzy and a full one for Chelsea before serving himself.

"Sandwich?" He handed the porcelain platter with the paper doily on it to Chelsea even though Mazzy's hand had snapped right out for the crustless peanut-butter-and-jelly triangle Frank, the cook, had grudgingly made.

"Yes, thank you." Chelsea's amber eyes sparkled and crinkled at the corners. She handed Mazzy a sandwich and a few small cookies before handing the platter back to him. "Thank you for having us to tea, also, Master Jack." She dipped her head and he felt like he was in one of those period films from England his sister used to make him watch.

"Yeah, thanks, Mister Big Man," Mazzy said through the cookie she had stuffed into her mouth.

He and Chelsea laughed together as she bent forward to wipe at her child's mouth with a linen napkin edged in royal blue. He caught a whiff of the fragrance in her hair and was thrown back in time. Lemons. She still used the shampoo that made her smell like lemons on a hot summer day.

He cleared his throat. "So, we have a lot of activities planned for the few days before the wedding and some I've put together for just the two of you."

Chelsea's eyes met his. "You didn't have to do that. I'm sure you're going to be busy yourself, and now that I have this wedding planner hat to wear, too, I might not have time."

"You're not wearing a hat, Mommy."

She tweaked Mazzy's nose. "You're right; it's just a figure of speech."

"What's that?"

"It means it's one more job I have to do. So you're going to be spending more time with Grammy than we originally planned."

"Yay! Grammy! She loves to see me." Another cookie got crammed into Mazzy's mouth and she spewed crumbs as she continued to talk. "She will make me cookies and pies and give me hugs and kisses."

Chelsea took a napkin from the table to give to her child. "I'm so sorry, Jack. If you'll tell me where the vacuum is, I can take care of that." She turned to her daughter. "Remember, we don't talk with our mouths full."

"Okay," the child said, her mouth still full.

Chelsea rolled her eyes, while she tried to stifle a laugh. "Good job."

Jack watched the interplay, marveling at the way she seemed to be able to float from one situation to another. Raising Mazzy solo couldn't be easy, especially without help nearby. His sister frequently depended on his mother to help out and would even more once her son or daughter came along. He'd heard Chelsea and her husband had divorced, that the man wasn't involved with them. Who did Chelsea have to depend on, living in that city hours away from her family?

He shook the question off, because it was none of his business, and went back to making idle conversation with his guests. They talked about the weather and the upcoming wedding, of course. When the subject of Mazzy's dance class somehow came up, she had to get up and show him a move or two, which almost lost him a vase on a side table, such was her enthusiasm.

Chelsea was horrified, but nothing bad had happened, so he told her not to worry.

Their time was coming to a close, he realized as the big grandfather clock in the foyer chimed out its deep stroke of the hour. The little girl was obviously struggling to keep her eyes open at this point, and he had to get back to work.

"Well, thank you for coming to high tea, my ladies," he said with a smile and a bow. "Dinner will be served at six, though, and we all should go take a rest for the afternoon before the festivities."

Mazzy cocked her head to the side and gave him a curious look. "You mean I should go take a nap?" she asked, getting right to the point.

He laughed because there was something so refreshingly straightforward about a kid. He had once thought he'd have several by now, but life hadn't turned out that way. "Yep." He tapped her nose and sent a wink in Chelsea's direction. "You and your mom should go lie down for a little bit. I think Frank, the cook, has something special brewing for dinner. You wouldn't want to miss out on it because you're too much of a sleepyhead."

As if to prove his point, her eyelids drooped, her head nodding to one side before she jerked back awake. "I'm not tired, though."

"Oh, I think you are." Chelsea helped the little girl out of her chair and headed for the steps to the second floor and their room. Mazzy didn't protest, and that told a lot, even to him, who hadn't known her long. Perhaps her mom would come back down so they could get some things done while Mazzy wasn't underfoot.

She must have read his mind. Chelsea looked over

her pretty shoulder and mouthed, "I'll be right back," to him before escorting the drooping child up the stairs.

High tea had been a success, though something he'd thought of off the cuff. When he'd seen Mazzy's lower lip quivering, he only knew he did not want to start out their week here with tears. His cousin's young daughter loved high tea and was about the same age, so the words had popped out of his mouth. He didn't regret it one bit, either, because a Mazzy meltdown had been averted and Chelsea had looked absolutely stunning. He'd tried very hard during high tea not to notice the way her eyes sparkled and how her laugh tugged at something in his gut. It hadn't helped. He had noticed all those things and more. Like the way her hair smelled like lemons and the way she had one dimple high on her cheek right underneath her left eye. It creased in the most beguiling way.

And he did not need to be beguiled, he thought, taking their things back to the kitchen. He had an inn to run, a staff who now counted on him. Even though they were only hosting Chelsea and Mazzy until the wedding, the following week they were booked solid.

He was devoted to the inn and everything it represented to him. His mom called him a workaholic, but that was the way he liked it. Which was why he needed to get his head back in the game. Not to mention this was Paige's oldest friend and he'd get his manly parts handed to him on a silver platter if he messed with her—Paige's words, not his.

An hour of playing to lift a little girl's spirits was fine, but his desk was probably overflowing with things to do now. He couldn't afford to lose his focus.

He had approximately twenty minutes to get

himself prepared to switch from tea host to business man, with not a second to waste. Heading for the kitchen first, he asked for something a little more substantial than the small crustless sandwich triangles they'd had with tea. Next he went to his room to change into jeans and a short-sleeved button-down shirt. He couldn't resist the urge to make sure his hair wasn't standing up all over the place.

Within ten minutes he was back downstairs and coming through the kitchen door into the main house when he saw a more relaxed Chelsea on the grand staircase. She had changed back into jeans, too, pairing them with a scooped neck T-shirt that flirted with her creamy cleavage.

"Did she go down okay?"

"I had to carry her the last few feet, so yes." She dragged her hand along the finish of the banister as she came down the last two steps. He'd never before been jealous of an inanimate object, but the urge hit him now.

He cleared his throat—and hopefully his stupidity in the process. "If you'd like to step into your new office, I had Adele set a few things up for you that Paige requested. Perhaps they'll make things easier, and then you can tell me what I can do to help."

Why was he finding it so hard to resist touching her satiny skin? He hadn't seen her in years. And he'd never thought of her quite that way before, during or after Paige's threat. She was Chelsea, a friend, a tag-along, a fixture in his life like his sister or his guy friends. He valued her friendship, even if it was over the Internet and newly resumed after years without a word between them, far more than he would value stealing a kiss or two before she left. He had a lot of important balls juggling in the air right now and could not afford to add a relationship with a woman, much less a woman with a child.

Still, he couldn't resist enjoying the way she walked into the room and spun in a circle with her arms out to her side.

"It's awesome," she said when she finally came to a standstill.

He had to agree. Adele had outdone herself in the few hours she'd had. The small secretary desk was organized with file holders, notepads, a desk blotter and a pen holder, making it into a real honest-to-goodness working desk. A swivel chair was tucked under the desk, and a phone sat on a table within reaching distance. Chelsea's laptop bag lay square in the middle of the desk. Adele had even thought to put a small clutch of flowers into an old Mason jar.

All the furniture had been moved back against the walls, creating space on the floor for the many boxes Belinda, Chelsea's sister, had been bringing over for weeks now. He knew they contained a multitude of things for the wedding, but he didn't know what. Honestly, he hadn't been brave enough to actually look.

"This is everything your sister brought over. I think she said she still had a few more things at home." He mentally checked off the twelve boxes sitting on the floor and the big tube of something standing up against the wall. "I had Adele leave the things that looked like supplies down here and stack them in the corner. Your other luggage is to your right because I didn't want to move anything only to find out I had moved it to the wrong place."

She squeezed his arm with a smile of pure gratitude. "You're the best, Jack." She took another glance around. "Should I put the things that go upstairs outside the door? Then I can just move them a few at a time, if that's okay. I'd like to wait until Mazzy wakes up, since I could really use the break and she needs the sleep."

"Anytime is good. In fact, let me know what you want where and I'll work on getting it there. I know you're taking on more than you thought you would. I'd like to help make it as easy as possible for you."

"I appreciate it. I don't have to tell you I've never done this before. I'm nervous it won't go right."

He stilled the hand fluttering around her neck by taking it in his own. "No, you don't have to tell me. But I will tell you this is going to be the best wedding in the history of weddings, and your sister will love it. No worries. Trust me. I've never let you down. Okay?"

"Okay." The tension went out of her shoulders. "I really do know how to do the organizational part. And Paige has me all set up with so many lists I'm sure there's one in there to remind me to brush my teeth on the big day. But this is so much bigger than making sure we have enough coffee and donuts for the annual shareholders' meeting."

Her laugh was nervous and a little bit self deprecating. It reminded him so much of the younger Chelsea he almost hugged her. Her lemony scent reached his nostrils again, reminding him of long, hot summer days spent at the lake and of building a tree house for two determined girls, a lifetime ago. He stepped away from her with some regret, but it was for the best. He didn't know what her personal life was like, but his was full enough without starting something that wouldn't be finished.

He dusted his hands together, getting back to work. "All right. Let's get these lists out and see what we can do to make sure everything goes according to plan. How long did you say Mazzy would be down for?"

"About two hours, if we're lucky."

"Then we'll hope our luck holds and go from there."

****

Chelsea was all too aware of Jack sitting behind her in an accent chair done in deep green. With a folder opened on his lap, she could hear the crackle of the pages he was flipping over one by one. He would ask a question every now and then, his deep voice seeming to sneak up on her even though by now she had heard it more times than she could count.

Why was she so aware of him, when he'd always just been the older brother all those years ago? She honestly had no idea—and no time to contemplate it. One week might seem like enough days to get everything ready, but given the copious notes in front of her she wondered if two years wouldn't be enough to get all this done in time for Belinda to be married without a thing out of place.

"Do you want me to make the phone calls Paige has set up for the various services leading up to the wedding day itself?" he rumbled. This time she didn't resist the urge to turn around. She found him exactly as she had imagined him to be a mere moment ago. His sleeves were pulled tight against his muscled biceps and his ankle was casually resting on the opposite knee. He didn't slouch but he looked comfortable, as if he had settled in for a long chat and had the time and patience to do whatever it took to get this right.

She, in contrast, was ready to jump out of her skin. This was terrible timing and a horrible location for her hormones to start taking notice, for the first time in a long time, that she was a woman.

"Um, yes, the phone calls would be great, if you don't mind. That way I can concentrate on making sure I have everything Paige has listed on this paper. I guess I'll find all the supplies I need in those boxes. Or at least I hope I will. You know how Belinda can be sometimes."

"Yeah, you don't have to remind me. I kid you not, she's called me about a thousand times since she chose the inn to have her wedding. Probably a million times before that, too."

He wasn't far off, so she laughed. Her sister had called her about three hundred times just for measurements for her bridesmaid dress. She never wanted to discuss the distance between her nipples again.

"She can be quite the go-getter. And that's the polite way of putting it."

"Mmmm."

She took the noise as an affirmative and turned back to her work when she saw he was deep into the paperwork, again, and making lists. She needed to find boxes of linens and tablecloths, turquoise napkins and lavender place cards. She had the lists from Paige that she now had to line up with the boxes from Belinda. Leaving the baby monitor on the desk so she could hear if Mazzy woke up, she went over to the boxes to the right of Jack's chair. Once she knelt down, she used the

Exacto knife he provided to pop open the first box. It had to be the right one, since mounds of tulle flowed out as if released from captivity.

Moving on, she opened another filled with fake trailing ivy and cut-crystal candleholders. She grabbed a thick black marker from the pen-stuffed glass jar on her new desk and began marking all the boxes with their contents. This way she wouldn't have to check each box every time she needed something. It was one of her strengths and one of the reasons the people at the big corporate office where she worked wanted her to step into the recently vacated position of executive secretary. She was ready to take on more responsibility, and the promise of more money was something she looked forward to.

Jack stood up from his chair to tower over her. "I think I'll check in with Frank. See if dinner is going to be on time. Then I'll make some of these calls. I'll leave you to your cataloging and see you for supper."

"Sounds good," she said, trying not to think about standing, too, and seeing if she really would fit right under the curve of his arm.

She watched him walk away again and barely stopped herself from drooling. He was yummy, no doubt about it, but this wasn't the right time or place. And it certainly wasn't the right man.

There was something to be said for having a person who knew you for a long time as a friend. But anything more than that and the magic would be killed. He had seen her at her worst and sometimes at her best. She still cared about him as a friend, which made it hard to understand why she was getting these fluttery feelings in her stomach when he was near. Or why it suddenly got hotter in the room when he looked at her with those penetrating blue eyes.

She did, however, acknowledge that she breathed a sigh of relief when he left. She had eight days until the wedding and many things to do in that time. They would hardly see each other once today was over and she and Mazzy were settled in.

Gratitude flooded through her when the baby monitor told her Mazzy was making stirring noises. Running up the flight of stairs, she escaped the room where she had felt so cozy sitting with Jack, just moments ago, as if no time at all had passed and nothing new was happening inside her. Nothing new, nothing new, she thought. She would continue with that mantra no matter how much she longed to go sit on his lap, scoot the papers out of his hand, and curl up away from the world.

****

Dinner that night was filled with great conversation and good food. Jack even broke his own rule and sat down at the guest table in the dining room with Mazzy and Chelsea. He hadn't had a sit-down dinner with anyone but his staff in too long to remember. After laughing at Mazzy's antics, he carried her up to bed for Chelsea when the little girl nearly fell asleep in her shepherd's pie.

"I can take her," Chelsea whispered in the dim light of the hallway on the second floor.

"That's okay, just lead me in and make sure nothing's in my way. I'll be fine." His precious cargo was not that heavy, but he had still climbed a whole set of stairs with her dead weight and would welcome setting her down.

Chelsea cleared the way as he had asked, then set about taking off Mazzy's shoes and socks. He turned to go, but she stopped him with a quiet word. "Wait. Please."

He did wait, in the next room, while she got her child ready for bed. He could already smell Chelsea in the room, that citrus scent that had seemed benign years ago now clung to him like a siren's song.

Fortunately, Chelsea entered the room before he could get too far down memory lane. She pulled the door to the extra room closed behind her, then walked closer.

"Do you have everything you need?" he asked, taking a few more steps toward the open door to the hallway. He might not have gotten too far down memory lane, but he had to watch his step. Nostalgia was one thing, and it was nice to have her here, but he'd always thought of her as a sister. That couldn't change.

"Yeah, thanks." She drummed her fingers on the top of the chest of drawers, which she had already made her own with some change, a few trinkets, and a set of earrings. "And thanks for hanging out with us at dinner tonight. I know you probably have a million things to do, but it was nice for Mazzy to have a man's attention for an hour or two. You went above and beyond the call of duty."

He brushed the compliment off. "It's not exactly a hardship, Chelsea. She's a great kid. You're lucky to have her."

"Yeah, I am. It's too bad Paul won't take the time to get to know her."

This was tricky territory he wasn't sure he wanted to tread. He knew her husband had left, but nothing more. Something in the tone of her voice told him things were not rosy. "I was sorry to hear about the divorce," he said, then winced. There was really no good way to say those words.

She moved from the chest of drawers to a post of the bed, grabbing hold and clutching it to her chest as if it were a lifeline. "Thanks."

She looked so sad he wanted to hug her. Back in the day, he probably wouldn't have hesitated. It wasn't an everyday occurrence, since she was Paige's friend, not his, but she'd had her heart broken a few times by jerks, and he'd given her a hug to get her through. However, it had been too many years and too many memories for him to get through that space between them. "Mazzy seems to be okay. Does she understand what happened?"

Chelsea didn't answer at first, which made him back up a step. He had gone too far. He should escape while he still could, with his feet on the ground instead of in his mouth.

"Don't go," she said as he put his hand on the door to leave. "I'm just trying to come up with a way to answer your question without painting myself like a total and complete idiot."

"You could never be an idiot."

"Spoken like a true friend." She smiled, the dimple under her eye coming out for a moment. "The truth of the matter is that I was an idiot. A complete and total one, no less. I kept thinking his not showing interest in her was normal for a guy when the baby is little. There's not much they do, and Paul was pretty active and busy. Why would he want to hang out with a baby who just drooled? But I loved her and thought I did enough with and for her. One day she would get older and start to talk and he would be interested in her. Show her some love."

He could guess the rest, but her eyes had taken on a faraway cast, as if she were reliving those moments while gathering the right words. She'd always been a doer to Paige's thinker. Maybe that had changed with single motherhood.

"So then he finished grad school. It was supposed to be his turn to work and take care of Mazzy while I went back to school to finish up my degree in chemistry. But after one week at home, he decided it wasn't going to work for him. He brought her to me at my job, took off for the ski slopes, and we haven't seen him since, no matter how many times I call."

She released her death grip on the post and swung back and forth with her hands clasped around the wood, mimicking Mazzy's swinging this morning. It was interesting to him that behavior could be passed down without ever being witnessed. When Mazzy had taken her turn this morning, he'd had a flashback of Chelsea doing the same thing when she was much younger. Now her hair wasn't as long. It didn't flow out behind her in a silky curtain. She looked to be lost in her own world, one not as happy as in younger days, but now not as sad as she had looked a moment ago, either.

"You know, I haven't told anyone the whole thing yet. No one at all. Even Paige only knows he won't come around but not how he left or when, exactly."

"Really?" He would have thought at least his sister would have the whole story.

"Really. They have parts and pieces. A truth here, a half-truth there, but no one has the whole unvarnished truth. Except you. You haven't changed much, except for the taller part, Jack. You're still the best listener."

She sounded almost wistful when she said that.

"But enough about me and my life. Any chance the bar in the speakeasy is open? I could use a glass of wine. I have the monitor, and Mazzy will be asleep for the night now."

"Sure." He'd just put off until tomorrow the other things he had to do. Make sure Chelsea knew she did have a friend in him. Though he'd always been the older brother to her, he'd still always been there for her and was not going to back away now. Especially because she looked like she needed someone to listen and not judge.

Any thoughts of how her lips looked soft enough to kiss or of scooping her up to hug her would just have to go to the place they had always been, locked up tight behind the door of friendship.

Chapter Three

Nerves assailed Chelsea's stomach as she stood outside the beautiful shop on Main Street in the next town over from the inn. Huge glass windows glinted in the midmorning sun. She held Mazzy's hand tight, afraid to step into the exquisite shop in case the little girl got out of hand and ran around like she had at Jack's.

"Now, Snazzy Mazzy, you have to be extra good in here, right?"

"Right. I'll be the bestest girl you've ever seen." The smile covered her whole face and made Chelsea just a little bit nervous.

"Please don't run around or touch anything you aren't allowed to touch, okay?"

"Got it, Mommy. I want to see all the pretty dresses!"

In no way, shape, or form was Mazzy out of control or a bad girl. She was a typical four-year-old, but Chelsea was the one who was worried. In their usual routine, when the little girl wasn't at the sitter's they'd stay at home or go out to do kid things. They frequented places like the local children's museum or a park where it was perfectly okay to run around and have fun. Paige had told her the women who ran Decadence were wonderful, but Chelsea still had bats careening around in her stomach.

"Are you going in, or were you just going to stand here and stare at the completely delicious-looking cake?" Belinda hooked an arm through Chelsea's and gave Mazzy a kiss on the cheek.

"We're going in, Aunt Belle, so I see all the pretty dresses."

"Well, hopefully mine will be the prettiest and so will yours."

"I bet they will be!" Mazzy danced on the sidewalk and was getting wound up.

"Best behavior," Chelsea warned.

"I know, Mom." Exasperation was clear in the child's voice, and Chelsea worried that she said those words too much.

But then she didn't have much time to worry about anything else because a tall blonde whisked open the door and ushered them into what was most aptly named Decadence.

"Moore party!" the woman hollered through the store, in sharp contrast to the soft jazz playing through hidden speakers.

"Yes!" Another blonde boogied out of a back room. She hit some switch and the music immediately went to the techno/trance that Belinda loved.

"Let's get this party started," a brunette contributed, coming in from the other side of the store, where the cakes were set out with mouthwatering goodness.

They introduced themselves and Chelsea was told that the first blonde, Claudia, did the cakes, the second blonde, Zoe, did the flowers, and May, the brunette, was the one who would make all of Belinda's dress dreams come true.

"I'm sorry my mom couldn't be here today," Claudia said. "I was going to have her take Mazzy under her wing and show her around while we fitted your dress."

"It's okay. She'll be fine," Chelsea answered.

Claudia bit her lip. "Would you mind her hanging out with a boy for a little while?"

Zoe nudged Claudia. "That is a fantastic idea. I'll go get him."

Chelsea felt caught up in a whirlwind but said yes. Mazzy would still be close. She was so used to taking care of her child on her own that she'd forgotten what it was like to have help.

"It'll be fine," Belinda whispered in her ear.

"Of course it will." Chelsea smoothed a hand over her daughter's head and hoped she was right.

A boy of about ten or eleven came into the shop, his hair flopping over his forehead, a ratty pair of sneakers on his feet. Claudia sighed and put her hand on her hip but then seemed to think better of whatever she was going to say and smiled, instead.

"Hey, Justin, can you hang with Miss Snazzy Mazzy here for a little while, so we can get these ladies in their dresses?"

Mazzy's face lit like a thousand light bulbs had been flicked on at the same time. "I brought coloring books, Justin!" she announced, and proceeded to drag him over to the tall bistro table in the cake area and chatter his ear off.

"Are you sure this is going to be okay?" Chelsea twisted her fingers together until Claudia placed a long-fingered hand over hers.

"It's going to be better than okay. It's going to be

fabulous, just like you when we get you into this dress. We'll fit Mazzy in a few minutes. Don't worry."

A loud laugh from Justin sounded over the music, and Chelsea watched as he patted Mazzy on the head. It was going to be fine.

May brought out Chelsea's dress first, and she stood for a second just admiring what she had only seen in pictures up until this moment. The square neckline sat above an empire waist that would flatter her figure and show off the arms she'd been trying to work on lately at the gym. Two darts had been made to conform the dress to her chest, and she was now thankful she had measured the distance between her nipples twice to get it right.

"If you want to step into the first room over here, we'll get you suited up first, so I can see what needs to be nipped and tucked." May hung the dress on the back of the door and ushered Chelsea into a plush room with a small loveseat and a leather-topped antique table.

Chelsea peeked her head out and made eye contact with Belinda, who just nodded at her and made shooing motions.

When had she gotten so paranoid? It wasn't as if they had never done anything outside their home before. While she didn't have a lot of friends where she lived, she certainly wasn't a hermit. There was something about being home, though, that made her not want Mazzy to get too used to this kind of togetherness.

She shook her head at herself in the mirror. She was being ridiculous, and the proof was in the fact that togetherness wasn't a bad thing. In fact, once she got the promotion she hoped to make this trip far more often. It would be good for Mazzy to have relationships here.

Sliding the dress over her head reminded her of the dress she'd worn the day before and how beautiful she'd felt in it. Special, if only for the short time she and Mazzy had tea with Jack. Another ridiculous thought. Because even if she came back here more often, she still wasn't ready to pursue anything more than friendship with him. He was mighty fine to look at, and a gentleman—very unlike her husband—but that didn't make him dating material.

And speaking of material, Belinda was calling from outside the door, threatening to come in if she didn't come out soon. Chelsea brushed the lines of the dress to make it fall at her bare feet the way it should and was stunned at how gorgeous it was. She'd only ever seen it in a catalog and online and had been afraid the color and cut would look terrible on her. She had been prepared to wear it regardless, because this was her sister's wedding, but instead she was amazed at how perfectly it suited her.

She stepped out of the dressing room to find her sister and the ladies from Decadence waiting for her.

"Oh, my gosh! Other than your dress, Belinda, I think that's the best thing I've ever created," May said, walking around Chelsea in a circle. "I don't think I need to do a single thing to it. What do you think, Claudia?"

"No, it's stunning. Great job, hon. I guess all those bowls of cereal didn't go to waste after all." The three owners of the shop laughed at what must have been an inside joke, and Chelsea felt herself deflate just a little. Other than Paige, she didn't have anyone she shared that kind of thing with.

And there she went sourpussing over choices she'd made and a life that was everything she wanted it to be. She just had to maybe think about getting out a little more and making it a point to find some friends. Nothing wrong with that. She would start working on it as soon as she got back to her apartment. Surely there was someone in the area who shared her like of Chinese food and movies with subtitles.

"Me next!" Mazzy came careening around a counter and nearly crashed into a pedestal with a huge crystal vase of flowers on it. Chelsea cringed and Zoe smiled.

"Hey there, flower girl," Justin said as he came in behind Mazzy. "I think you forgot to get your walking shoes."

Mazzy laughed and stared up at Justin as if he'd made the world. Oh, lordy, her first crush.

"You have to stay right here, Justin, while I try on my dress. I'll be right back." And Mazzy marched into the fitting room, calling for her dress like a monarch.

May was all too happy to oblige. Chelsea just stood there for a moment, feeling the dress on her skin, the smile on her face, and the peace of the store. It was definitely a great place to be, and soon she would get to see her sister in her dress. Their mother should be here any moment, and then poor Justin would be overwhelmed with estrogen. But he looked like he was fine with that. If she remembered correctly, Claudia had raised her child all alone and seemed to have done a fine job of it. No saying that Chelsea couldn't do the same. Of course Claudia had probably had her whole family around her, but that was just how it happened sometimes.

Mazzy came prancing out in a lilac dress. It fit her adorably as she spun in a circle, flashing eyes at Justin every time she came back around to him. Chelsea had a feeling it was going to be all about Justin for the next few hours.

In the next dressing room, Chelsea removed her dress, carefully put it back on the hanger, and redressed before stepping out of the room. It gave her a little time to resettle herself again. This was all a good thing, and having Mazzy here would give the child more sense of place when she talked to her grandparents now. And for herself, perhaps it would make her want to call everyone more often. These, too, were not bad things.

She helped Mazzy redress in the next dressing room, and, sure enough, the conversation was all Justin and how he was Mazzy's new hero and best friend in the whole wide world. She wasn't very quiet about it, either. When they stepped out of the room, Justin's ears were beet red, but he was game to take her back to the table where they had sat before and get her into coloring once more.

At that moment, Chelsea's mother walked in, and the whole place filled with cheer because it was finally Belinda's turn. Chelsea surreptitiously looked around to make sure Leigh hadn't trailed any of the threatened bachelor parade in behind her. Seeing no men, she breathed a sigh of relief as May stepped into a corner dressing room to help Belinda.

Claudia pulled Chelsea aside. "Listen, if there's anything you need, anything at all while you're here, please make sure to let us know," she said.

"Of course."

"No, now, come on, I really mean that. Jack might

be a hunk, but he's not always savvy about the girl thing. So, really, if you need some girl time, or some alone time, or help with anything, seriously, let us know. Justin has taken quite a shine to your little girl, and she's adorable. If you run into any snafus with the caterers or the spa or whatever, I have connections, so don't be afraid to call me."

"I really will, and thank you." It was so tempting to tell this woman about how she felt being near Jack again, but they didn't know each other well. Maybe that was part of the lure. But if she wasn't ready to tell Belinda, then she shouldn't tell anyone. Normally, she'd tell Paige, but since Jack was her brother that could get messy.

Not that there was really anything to tell. Lord, she was going to drive herself crazy. Today was for Belinda and that was all.

Making a quick phone call to let Paige know they were good to go on dresses, she hung up the phone before she could blurt out her stupidity and ruin a good thing. The week would be up soon enough, and she'd be back outside Philadelphia with her child and her promotion, and it would be enough. She'd make sure of it.

****

Finishing up his shopping, Jack hoped everything was going according to plan back at the inn this afternoon. He'd dropped by the DJ to hand over the rest of the new list Belinda had put together. He'd also visited the manicurist, the hairdresser, and the spa to make sure all the appointments set up for later in the week were still a go. He could have just called them, but he much preferred the personal touch. As a bonus, it was also easier than trying to convince himself not to stare at Chelsea's fine form when he should have been concentrating on the list of table seatings Paige and Belinda had come up with. The girls had fittings at Decadence this morning, and that would run into the afternoon. And he had been told to expect more people for dinner.

All his errands done, he headed back to the inn he had called his for the last three years. His father had handed the keys to him and wished him well two years to the day after he'd graduated from college with his hospitality degree. He'd been running the place for the year before, but his dad made it official on that day, saying, "It's time your mom and I take a turn at enjoying someone else's hospitality." Jack had never been prouder than on that day. He had only hoped at the time that he hadn't taken on more than he could handle.

With Adele and Frank as fulltime staff, and the others who were willing to jump in for extra things, he had never been more sure than now that he was going to make this place a success. He'd like to share that success with someone more intimate and had recently started thinking about settling down, but it would have to be with someone who loved the inn as much as he did. An image of Chelsea in the dark purple dress at high tea flashed into his mind. He shook his head to dispel the image and the crazy thought. Chelsea was not that person, and he shouldn't even be thinking about her that way.

Yes, she was beautiful and sweet, and her daughter was a hoot, but he needed someone local, someone who would be fine with devoting themselves to the inn and making it a success.

"Preferably someone I've known over the last eight years better than for just a few shared email exchanges and two meals," he said into the quiet of the car as he shook his head at himself.

As he drove through the small town of Kissinger, it began to rain softly. Perfect. The bride had wanted natural flowers around the arbor where they would say their vows. Now she would have them, as long as the rain stayed soft and stopped before it got too muddy.

When he pulled up to the house, he had to park around back because it looked like everyone who was supposed to be here had arrived. He grabbed his one grocery sack out of the back seat of his sedan, then nudged the door shut with his knee.

The kitchen smelled of roasted chicken and savory bread. Frank stood over the stove like a man doing war with pots and pans. The guy had been in the military until last year, when he mustered out after thirty years. Needing a job because he couldn't handle all the idle hours, he'd come to Jack with his experience in running the galley on huge aircraft carriers. Once Jack had encouraged him to start using more spices, the guy had gone from good to gourmet.

Pots and pans boiled and sizzled on the island range. Steam rose thick in the air when Frank opened the oven to remove the fragrant bread. It looked like chaos in here, but Jack knew it was organized chaos. The faster he got out of the thick of things, the faster they could get on with the business of dinner. Chelsea had called him on his cell phone while he was out and asked if some of the women could come over for dinner so she didn't have to go around to all of their houses. He hadn't said no, of course. But that necessitated a visit to the grocery store tucked in with his other errands.

Glancing at the enormous rooster clock on the far wall, he did a double take. He hadn't realized it was so late. Putting the bag of last-minute necessities on the butcher block, Jack turned—and almost bowled over Chelsea on his rush to get out into the dining room.

Her hair was pulled up in a topknot and her eyes were just this side of wild.

"What happened?" He looked for injuries and was about to go get Mazzy to see if she was all right when Chelsea gripped his arm with surprising strength.

"I need your help."

"Anything. You name it, it's yours."

"You might regret that when you hear what I want you to do."

He highly doubted it, but he wasn't stupid enough to go in totally blind. "Okay, name it and I'll most likely be able to make it happen." He smiled, but she didn't return the gesture.

"I just told my mom that we're engaged. Can you pull that off for the week?"

Thank God the counter was directly behind him. He gripped the beveled edge as a million thoughts raced through his brain. First and foremost was what in the world was he supposed to say to that?

"Look, I know this is coming out of left field and way too much to ask, but pretty please? With sugar on top and cherries and my first born?"

"Uh." Not intelligent at all. Her eyes were getting a little wilder, but this wasn't them daring each other to see who could jump the farthest into the creek.

"Please just say yes, and we can work out all the

details later."

Frank started whistling over at the stove. Jack's ears went hot. What was he supposed to do?

"You said anything was mine."

Now those wild eyes had started taking on a sheen he did not like. "Okay, but is your mother really going to believe that?"

"She will. I'll make her believe it."

"And why are we making her believe it?" He pulled at his collar because the damn thing had shrunk two sizes.

"Because I refuse to be a part of the bachelor parade."

"Um, okay. But what about Mazzy?"

"She's not going to be a part of the bachelor parade either."

"I can't pretend that I know what you're talking about, but if this is what you need, then I guess I can be game."

She chewed on her bottom lip. He should back out now instead of going through with this ridiculousness. Whatever a bachelor parade was, it couldn't be good. But he couldn't stand to see her in this kind of distress even if the only result he could see was him ending up the loser.

"Let me worry about Mazzy. I'll think up something. I just have to make it through dinner and then it will all be good."

"Are you sure?"

Straightening her shoulders, she looked him right in the eye. "I am positive. Now make sure you play the doting fiancé this week. I'll make excuses for tonight's dinner, but after that we'll be on. My mother will never be able to keep her mouth shut." She swiped a hand over her forehead. "We apparently fell in love over the Internet. Either that or we've been in love this whole time and just couldn't admit it to ourselves. Take your pick."

He watched her turn on her heel and stalk back through the swinging kitchen door.

Frank's whistling stopped mid tweet. "Boss man?"

Jack raised his hand. "Apparently I'm engaged." He rolled the word around on his tongue, and it felt both warm and foreign. What the hell had he agreed to?

"I'll take out the gravy as soon as possible."

"See that you do." He aborted his idea of joining the ladies for dinner and instead went up the back stairs to his rooms on the third floor. He tried hard not to think of Frank's snicker or the fact that his plan to stay away from Chelsea except when necessary wasn't going to work if they were now engaged. This could be a very long week.

****

"So anyway, your father says he's lost without me and couldn't find the peanut butter to make his own humble dinner." Chelsea's mother plopped an elbow on the table and dropped her head into her hand. "I can't believe he thinks that's going to work with me."

Chelsea's cousin Abby took a sip of her water. "That's nothing. I made a meal for Jon and he says he doesn't know how the microwave works to heat it back up. So he decided to just go out for a bite to eat with his buddies at the firehouse. He's full of crap, though. You should see—and taste—some of the meals they make down at the firehouse." She rolled her eyes. "And he's one of the chief cooks."

"Well, Marcus is completely set," Belinda said from Chelsea's left. "He knows his way around a kitchen, and we went grocery shopping for plenty of supplies before I left. But he still says he can't wait to have me with him all the time. Isn't that wonderful?" She admired her engagement ring, preening a bit.

Chelsea kept hoping Jack would come out soon and help her, despite the fact she'd told him to stay away. Then again, perhaps if he didn't come out she could keep the subject of her supposed engagement off the table entirely.

Jack hadn't exactly been excited about the prospect of pretending he'd fallen in love with her after all these years, but she couldn't fault him. It wasn't as if she'd even given him time to think it over. Heck, she hadn't taken the time to think it over, either. But as conversation swirled around the table, she realized what a huge mistake she had made. She'd asked her mother to keep the news to herself, saying she didn't want to overshadow Belinda's big day. But that, along with everything else she'd said, was a big lie. Lying made her uncomfortable, as a rule, but she hadn't known what else to say when her mother showed up early and confirmed that she had eligible men lined up for almost every function for the coming week. She'd also crowed about how she had several eligible bachelors she'd talked Belinda into inviting to the wedding so Chelsea could have her pick.

In response, Chelsea had blurted out, without a moment's hesitation, the story about falling for Jack over the course of the last month during their email exchanges. Why, oh, why hadn't she kept her mouth shut? It wasn't like being forced to meet eligible men would have been the end of the world. But she'd popped out the lie without thinking beyond her panic to get her mom to stop matchmaking, and now she was stuck with it.

Yeah, now she was totally stuck with it, unless she wanted to admit she'd lied. Her head hurt just thinking about all the complications of that particular conversation.

Belinda laughed about something and Chelsea joined in, though she had no idea what had been said. She put more gravy on her rice because she had nothing to add to the conversation. Did Jack know how to cook? Or did he rely on Frank to do all that while he ran the inn? What all was involved in running the inn? What did he do all day? Since she'd been here, he'd taken reservations and kept things spruced up, but what else was there to do? She had never been interested in that aspect of things when she'd been growing up at the inn with Paige. It was a place to play, but to Jack it had always been the place to be unless he was running Paige and Chelsea around at the request of his parents.

She scooped more rice. There was so much she didn't know about him. How would she convince her mother they were in love if she didn't know basic things about him? Perhaps her mother wouldn't really ask, and it was only for a week.

But she caught the tail end of Belinda telling the story of Marcus proposing, and the look her mother aimed at Chelsea told her there would be many questions and plans in the future. Her mother was a wonder at multitasking, and there was no doubt she would think she could start planning Chelsea's wedding now, even while Belinda's was also going on.

"So what do you have planned for us this week, Chelsea?" Belinda asked, bringing Chelsea back to the table and away from her worries.

She ran the listing through her head, the one that Paige had laid out on a spreadsheet with the precision of an accountant. "We'll be at the spa, have manicures, pedicures, hair dressing."

"But what about games? I know about all of that. I want together time. We hardly ever get to see you, and I want to hang out with you and do stuff before I turn into the bridezilla you all think I am."

Chelsea switched to the activities list in her mind. "Bridal shower. Attendants' tea. Bachelorette party."

"Naughty Bachelorette party?" Abby asked, with a twinkle in her eye.

"Not that naughty," Chelsea's mom said. "I won't be here, but we don't want to rock Jack's boat. He might not like that kind of thing going on in his house, with Chelsea here."

Her heart stopped when everyone looked at her.

"Why not? What's going on that he would mind you having some strippers in here?" Belinda quirked an eyebrow and leaned forward in her chair to the point where Chelsea was afraid she'd fall off.

"There's nothing going on." Chelsea cut a look at her mother. "I just think with Mazzy here and with the kind of establishment Jack is running we shouldn't have a male stripper show up. It will still be fun, and I promise a bit of naughty, but not that naughty. Okay?"

Belinda resituated herself in her chair, but she kept giving Chelsea the raised eyebrow, and Chelsea could almost see the wheels spinning in her sister's head. She'd have to be quicker on her feet and have another conversation with her mother about the absolute need for silence about this. She did not want to overshadow Belinda's big day and most surely not with what was in reality a lie.

"Anyway, I have a very special project everyone is going to be involved in for you, Belinda, and I'm not going to tell you anything more about it." That, of course, piqued Belinda's curiosity and fortunately derailed the quirked eyebrow. Thank goodness.

Once everyone cleared their plates, she ushered them down into the speakeasy. Exposed beams alternated with white paint on the low ceiling. Two tall pub-style booths sat against one wall, and the other walls were filled with a video game from the eighties, an old upright cooler in stoplight red, and a dart board. She had loved the times when Paige's dad would tell them stories about how the speakeasy had been a hub of activity back in the 1920s and 1930s, when people weren't legally allowed to drink in this county. But one of Jack's enterprising relatives hadn't let that stop him from imbibing or letting his friends imbibe.

If she could keep the conversation off her completely, that was the best way to go about things. Even though she had told Jack about Paul and his neglect, she did not want to rehash it this week with anyone else, and she had nothing more to say about Jack that wouldn't show her fake hand. She was giving herself a headache with all the things she couldn't talk about.

"Glasses of wine for everyone, even you, Chelsea," Belinda said, once they arrived in the pub-style basement.

"I'll drink to that." Abby said. "You need to loosen

up, Chelsea. Everything will go off without a hitch, and that adorable daughter of yours is going to be a beauty at the wedding. If you need any help, though, you just let me know. I didn't take the week off work, since I work part-time, but I am available if you need me."

More offers of help. While Chelsea appreciated them from the bottom of her heart, it brought her situation back at home into stark focus. She did not need that right now.

She smiled and thanked Abby, then broke out the wine from behind the bar where Jack had showed her it rested. With glasses arranged between her fingers like a real hostess, she brought it all to the table, where she poured with a flourish and then raised her glass with everyone else. "To Belinda—if Marcus lived through your flaws from your teenage years, this marriage thing is going to be a breeze!"

****

The sounds of a half dozen women laughing drifted up the stairs to the first floor where Jack was in the process of dimming the lights for the evening. It was good to have more youthful sounds ringing through the house again. His parents had made the inn a destination for the older crowd and he enjoyed them, but new blood in the place was excellent for business.

Turning the dimming switch in the library to a low point, he listened with a smile as a loud burst of mirth rose through the floor. It was a good thing Mazzy was on the second floor or she might have been awakened.

Adele had gone down into the speakeasy about thirty minutes ago to make sure the ladies had all the wine they needed. And then he'd sent her up to the rooms she used on the third floor, knowing they were going to be doing a lot of work over the next week and both needed rest. He'd assigned her the morning hours and had taken the evening himself. This week they were more than a bed and breakfast, since they would be providing all meals for Chelsea and Mazzy and a few for the rest of her family. Instead of having the majority of the day free, he and Adele would be working almost twenty-four hours a day.

And now he was also going to have to pull off being an engaged man. God, he didn't know what cork had come loose in his head to make him say yes to her request. But something about her eyes shining with her heartfelt request had made it seem easy enough. He couldn't think of anyone else he would have said yes to, and that made him nervous on a level he wasn't willing to contemplate.

But the ramifications… He couldn't think about that now. He had to go downstairs and at least show his face. This was his inn, after all.

So far the group had seemed very nice and undemanding. He'd known them all since he was a boy, but you never knew what you were going to get when someone was at your place of business. People changed when you were at their beck and call, but not the Moores. Adele had told him they'd enjoyed dinner and made a special point of thanking Frank for his hard work.

Jack wasn't necessarily counting on things remaining so nice. Some brides could turn into absolute beasts when the day got closer. He'd known Belinda as long as he'd known Chelsea, but not as well. From what he did know, he wouldn't put it past her. She'd been a hellion when they were younger. Chelsea had talked endlessly about her behavior, primarily with Paige, and with him by extension.

Worry about that could wait until, if and when, it came time. For right now he should go down and do his host duties, make sure they had everything they needed, then head for bed himself. Hopefully all while avoiding questions about how he'd proposed to Chelsea and when they were going to set a wedding date.

Straightening one last pillow, he left the library and headed for the staircase leading into the basement. But this was not a basement like most people had. Back in the days of Prohibition it had been a working speakeasy catering in secret to the dry county. His parents had restored it to its former glory with pub-style booths and a mahogany bar they'd imported from Ireland.

Jack had made the decision to not change a single thing when he became owner. He'd even added some things he'd collected from the two trips he'd taken to Ireland when he was younger, visiting his grandparents before they passed away. He'd also inherited some of their effects and incorporated them into the décor.

Descending the stairs, he was greeted by another burst of laughter. This was either a very merry bunch or a very drunk bunch. He'd bet a little of both.

Taking the last steps more quietly, he observed the group of beauties. There was the bride. He'd met her when she'd had no hair, a squalling infant long ago. Beside her, squeezed onto the two-person bench, were two other very pretty women who looked enough like her to know they were related. He knew them from high school.

He couldn't see Chelsea, her aunt, or her mother on the other side of the booth because of how tall the back was, but he had a clear picture in his mind of each of them. The aunt was nice when he saw her around town, but he only knew her well enough to say hello in passing. Mrs. Moore, however, had always been friendly to him, and when he was young she'd given him a place to hang out if the inn was overrun with guests. She had been a staunch supporter of his taking over the inn and had even sent several people his way. He didn't know her all that well as an adult, since they hadn't done much more than wave in passing before Belinda decided to have her wedding here, but he still had very fond memories of her chocolate chip cookies and the way she made a house a home. Something he'd been striving to do here at the inn. His parents had made it a destination and Jack wanted to take it back down to a home away from home. Neither way was wrong, but he wanted intimate and returning guests, not fly-byers. And he was going to have to lie to Leigh Moore's face when she asked about their engagement.

Curiosity more than anything propelled him to walk farther into the room to where he could catch a glimpse of Chelsea. He'd seen her in the kitchen, but her question had made him blind to anything but her pleading eyes. How would she look dressed up like everyone else—not in a formal gown and not in her jeans? He stopped at the bar and brought another bottle of wine with him, just in case they were in need of one. No use denying it was also a prop to hide the fact he should have left when he realized they were fine on their own.

He almost bobbled the bottle when he got a good look at the woman sandwiched between the aunt of the bride and Grammy.

Suddenly he was seventeen years old at a camp in upstate New York for the summer as a counselor to kids who were there for eight weeks. Paige and Chelsea, at fifteen, had signed up for it together, and his mom had encouraged him to go, too, since they might need looking after. It would look good on his resume and college applications, she'd said, but he had a feeling she just didn't want to let her little Paige out of her sight without someone to take over the watching. Chelsea and Paige had been inseparable in those days. What one did, so did the other. And as often was the case, he got volunteered to keep an eye on them. Not that he'd minded in the least that summer, since something about Chelsea had changed and flipped the switch from his little sister's best friend to a budding beauty.

The counselors had signed on for the eight weeks with campers plus one before and one after to open and close down the camp. On the last night, there had been a dance for the staff, and he had finally stolen a kiss from the girl he had followed around like a puppy dog for those ten weeks. Chelsea Moore had filled his dreams that summer.

He shook his head once to dispel the image. Chelsea Moore was no longer that same girl. Many years and many events separated them into the friendly strangers they were now. She had an incredibly adorable four-year-old daughter and a home and a life three hours from here. Not to mention a promotion coming her way. And she was still his sister's best friend, which made any interest on his part a huge no-no in Paige's book.

How did she plan on explaining their break-up when it came time for her return to her normal life, where she wasn't fakely engaged to him? Had she told Paige? Was she going to have a fit, or play along knowing it wasn't real?

Ignoring his own uneasiness, he waited for the laughter to die down before he said, "So, ladies, how is everyone? I hope you're settling in comfortably. The Barton Inn and the staff are here for your convenience."

Everyone smiled and thanked him. Chelsea's hair had been pulled up into a ponytail and she looked more like that fifteen-year-old girl than ever. Especially when she winked at him and mouthed thanks.

She sent his heart into a gallop with that one look. Red danger flags zoomed up in his head. His heart couldn't take this kind of blow. She was a sucker punch waiting to happen.

****

There was something in Jack's eyes when she mouthed thanks and winked at him that made Chelsea fluttery inside. She shoved the feeling down deep with all the other inappropriate things she had been feeling the last two days. She was still on the mend from a bad relationship, she told herself. Paul hadn't broken her heart because he didn't love her anymore—that had gone out the window six months after Mazzy was born—but he had broken her heart for her little girl. Chelsea was still on the healing part of the mend. It had been over two years since he'd left, but she was not ready to change anything more in her life.

And now she was going to have to act as if she and Jack couldn't be without each other. She'd dug a hole and dragged him into it. Her mother kept winking at her and nudging her. It wouldn't be long until Leigh Moore blabbed.

Before Chelsea was ready for him to leave, Jack waved, then turned back toward the stairs. At the bottom of the steps, he turned back with an adorably sheepish smile on his face. "I guess I should leave this with you all." After depositing the bottle in the middle of the table, he walked away with his hands tucked into his pockets.

"Now that is something to watch," her cousin Melanie said with a low whistle.

Horrified Jack might have heard her comment, Chelsea's eyes flew to Jack's retreating back. But his step didn't hesitate at all. Which hopefully meant he hadn't heard. Lord, wouldn't that have been embarrassing?

"I can't believe you said that!" Chelsea dropped back against the booth and glowered at her mother, who was snickering.

"I notice you immediately took a second look," Leigh said, nudging her with an elbow. "And he's all yours to look at now, honey."

"Mom!"

"Well, it's true, isn't it?"

"What does that mean?" Belinda asked, leaning forward with a keen look in her eyes.

"Nothing?" Chelsea asked.

"I doubt that." Belinda smirked. "Something you want to tell us, sister dear?"

"No."

"Liar. Spill."

"We really should work on some final details of your wedding, if you want to call me tomorrow?" Chelsea tried to scoot her mother out of the booth so she could run to her room. Leigh wasn't budging, and

Belinda grabbed Chelsea's hand before she could slide under the table.

"I like avoidance. It gives me the chance to pry it out of you."

Chelsea rolled her eyes. Now she'd done it. She had set her sister on the trail and there would be no appeasing Belinda until Chelsea came out with the answers her sister wanted. She decided to blurt it out like ripping off the wax on her eyebrows. "Jack and I are engaged. I didn't want to ruin your special time, so I was trying to keep it to myself until after your wedding." The lie tasted like ash in her mouth, but it rang in her head for just a moment as she saw herself walking down the aisle to Jack...living in this house...

Sure enough, everyone jumped in on the conversation, wedging her more securely into her lie and the booth.

"He's a great guy," her aunt said.

"I think he's yummy and that you are one lucky woman. Who wouldn't want that to come home to and snuggle up with?" Melanie chimed in.

"Melanie!"

"What? It's true." Melanie slid her a sly grin. "Maybe the two of you can christen every room here, now that you're together."

"Not going to happen. And even if it did, I wouldn't tell you," Chelsea said, feeling stuck between her mother and her aunt. The urge to get up and pace was nearly overwhelming her.

"All right, girls," Leigh said, patting Chelsea on the arm. "Let's all settle down. Chelsea wanted to keep this a secret, so we'll wait until after the wedding to razz her. I guess I'll have to uninvite all those eligible men,

Belinda."

They laughed, and Chelsea's stomach clenched. If only it had occurred to her to tell her mom she was engaged to someone back in Bettleton who couldn't pull himself away from his law practice or the many surgeries he had scheduled.

Well, at least the bachelor parade was one less thing she'd have to worry about. She wouldn't be dodging a few dozen men as her mother lobbed them at her one at a time.

"Have you told Mazzy yet, dear?" Leigh asked.

God, no. Her stomach knotted itself like a hangman's noose. The little girl was already following Jack around like a shadow. She would not involve her child in the lie she'd gotten herself stuck in.

"Not yet. Jack and I were planning on having a dinner the day after Belinda's wedding to announce it to our friends and family. I'll tell Mazzy then." Of course they would have broken up by then, so there was no need to go there. The lie was just getting bigger and bigger.

"That makes sense, I guess. I'm so excited for you, though, and want to know all the details. Mazzy is going to look so adorable as your flower girl, especially since she has my wedding to practice at. I hope I can keep my mouth shut," Belinda said.

"Then let's stop talking about it now so we can concentrate on you and your day. We have manicures and pedicures, outings and picnics planned."

"You might be trying to change the subject, sister dear, but I can only be distracted for so long." Belinda smiled with all her teeth.

Chelsea didn't care if she had to do loop-de-loops

and handstands as long as they could move from Jack to other, more comfortable subjects. Eventually she did manage to distract them all with talk about the upcoming wedding and the activities scheduled to keep them busy and make them beautiful on the lead-up to the big day.

But that night, after tiptoeing across her room to Mazzy's and checking on her daughter through the connecting doorway, she couldn't get the image of a grown-up Jack out of her mind.

With his dark hair, broad back, and mouthwatering body, he'd filled out in a way that made her woman's heart beat just a little bit faster. If her mother's heart wasn't so much the dominant part of her these days, she might have appreciated more how very yummy he now was.

However, the little girl in the room next door needed her more than any man ever would. And Chelsea needed her daughter to be happy, healthy, and loved. All things she herself could and did provide by herself.

She'd tried the two-parent family with Mazzy's dad for the first two years and it hadn't worked out. Once his degree was done, he had told her he wasn't staying around anymore. The love was gone and he had other things he wanted to do, another life he wanted to live that didn't include them. And then he had completely ignored them. Oh, he still sent child support checks, but she had wanted him to be involved, to love her little girl as much as she did, and she couldn't leave Bettleton before that had a chance to happen. Mazzy deserved to know her father even if Chelsea couldn't convince him to give her the time just yet.

Mazzy knew she had a father, in a general way, that she hadn't been pulled out from under a cabbage. Chelsea had been careful not to lie to her, but she hadn't told her the whole truth, either. For being four, Mazzy didn't have many questions about where this father was and why he wasn't around. Chelsea was braced for the day that would happen, though. Hopefully, she could talk Paul into being a part of Mazzy's life before it became necessary to explain something Chelsea herself couldn't fathom. How did you not love the being you'd created?

She could not, and would not, subject her little girl to another person walking away from her. Especially now when Mazzy was old enough to understand when the person said he loved her and wanted to see her grow up—and then be hurt when he did neither.

Chelsea flopped back onto the bed with her arms spread out, taking up as much room on the queen-sized bed as possible. This was all hers and would always be all hers. She did not have to share her life with anyone but Mazzy, she did not have to share her bed with anyone unless Mazzy crept in, and she would not share her heart with anyone but Mazzy, ever again.

It was as simple, and as complicated, as that.

Trouble falling asleep was nothing new to Chelsea, but she made the effort. The hustle and bustle would continue tomorrow. She needed proper rest if she hoped to keep up with her sister and their two cousins. They could probably run circles around her when it came to self-indulgence.

There were massages and shopping and manicures and spa days to look forward to in the coming days. All things Chelsea normally would not do for herself but had agreed to do here because her sister was the bride and had demanded it. Chelsea wasn't necessarily against any of the activities. They just didn't fit into her normal life or budget as a secretary.

But this would be fun, she told herself, hoping she would believe it when she was dragged all over creation and plastered and waxed to within an inch of her life.

If nothing else, hopefully it would get her thoughts away from what it would be like to really be engaged to the handsome and charming Jack.

Chapter Four

This was never going to work. Chelsea walked around the library at the inn, circulating among family and old friends alike. The staff at Barton Inn had laid out a stunning array of cheese and crackers, fruits and vegetables, on clear glass trays rimmed with gold and garnished with flowers from Jack's gardens. While it all looked appetizing, Chelsea had only taken a little from each offering, for show. No way would she be able to actually stomach anything.

Any minute now someone would grill her on her engagement. What would she say? Would she be able to pull off looking at Jack with her proverbial heart in her eyes? He was easy enough to look at, but that didn't translate into being gaga over him to the point of supposedly accepting his never-uttered proposal. She was an idiot. She should have never started this in the first place.

It was on the tip of her tongue to ding her glass and just announce that she and Jack had been playing a prank. But she had no idea who actually knew what at this point. She would make a fool out of herself if she blurted out that it was a lie before anyone was actually aware of the lie in the first place. It was only Monday and she was already regretting the snap decision.

A hand landed on her shoulder, the warm palm sending minute shudders throughout her system. "Are you having a good time, darling?"

"Don't lay it on thick," she whispered out of the corner of her mouth.

Jack's laugh rumbled through her. "I'll try to hold myself back," he whispered in her ear.

She smiled, but it was strained around the edges. Hopefully no one else would notice.

"Jack!" Leigh, Chelsea's mother, carefully picked her way through the crowded library to give him a big hug. Here it came. Her mother leaned in as if conspiring, which she probably was. "I know we're not supposed to tell anyone," she said softly enough that no one but Chelsea and Jack could hear. "I just wanted to congratulate you, though, and say how excited I am that you'll finally be a part of our family. I hope this means you're going to participate in this week's activities more than just as the proprietor of the inn."

Now Jack's smile was the one a tad strained around the edges. Chelsea hadn't even thought that far ahead. What she would have given to be able to smack herself in the head without anyone noticing. The fake guy in Bettleton would have been so, so much easier, if only she'd been quicker on her toes with her mother. This was never going to work.

That warm palm settled on Chelsea's shoulder again, dissipating the rising tension. How did he do that?

"I will be a part of as many things as possible, Leigh," Jack said in the same hushed voice. "I know how important this wedding is to your family, and I don't want to overshadow it with our news. You understand, I'm sure. But you can count me in for as many festivities as I can get away for. Now, I should go make sure the kitchen's ready to serve lunch. If you'll excuse me?" He leaned in to kiss Chelsea on the cheek and give her the moon eyes. They looked good on him. Far better than she could have pulled off.

She watched him walk away, all six-plus feet of him, and made an effort to look smitten. Thankfully, she must have pulled it off. Her mom put an arm through hers and cackled with glee.

"I knew this would happen sooner or later! You two were meant for each other. All those days you and Paige ran around together while growing up and being shepherded around by Jack were bound to come to something." Her mom kissed her on the cheek opposite from where Jack's kiss still simmered. "I'm so happy for you. And so is your dad, though he's not entirely pleased Jack didn't ask our permission," she chided.

Chelsea almost swallowed her tongue. But she got it back into the proper place long enough to say, "It was kind of a sudden thing. I can ask Jack to go over to see Dad when this is all over, if Dad wants him to." And wouldn't that be the height of awkwardness? She could see Hugh Moore now, asking Jack why he wanted to marry his daughter, and Jack floundering because, really, what reason could he give?

"The deed is already done, dear. That's okay. We're just so pleased you're going to be coming back home. We'll be able to see our Mazzy more. How long are we talking as far as a long engagement? I don't want to wait a year to have my Snazzy Mazzy all to myself. I want to see the ring, too. I know you're trying to be discreet, but your sister's wedding shouldn't keep you from showing off your sparkler."

Chelsea had to get away. She had not thought this

whole thing through and now she was stuck. But she could not stand with her mother one more minute without fixing it. And if she told the truth, not only would her mother be angry with her, but the promised bachelor parade would be back on.

"I'm going to see what I can do to help Jack." She slipped her arm out from under her mother's.

"Hopefully, you can also steal a kiss while you're in the kitchen." Leigh winked and sighed. "True love is a beautiful thing. I'm so glad you finally found it."

Scurrying away, Chelsea couldn't help but think how inept she was at lying. Despite how things ended with Paul, she had been in love with him when they'd first married. Apparently her mother thought it hadn't ever been true love. So if she hadn't been convincing the first time, when it was real, then how was she going to pull off pretending to be head over heels in love with someone she was struggling to remember she was only fond of as an old friend? This week couldn't go fast enough.

****

Jack had to get his head on straight. He stood in the middle of the bustling kitchen, staying out of everyone's way as best he could. His rooms upstairs would have been a better option, but he couldn't leave his staff hanging just because he was having a personal crisis.

"Get those plattered," Frank said from behind him, bringing him out of not only his fantasies but his worries.

"I've got it." Jack had spent many an evening and most summers doing kitchen duty. His parents had run a well-received bed and breakfast, but it had never seen an event like this. Usually it was a destination for a few people to spend the night or a getaway for a couple. They had five guest rooms, total, so the meal load was often less than twelve, and only breakfast at that. This was a whole new thing. One Jack was enjoying while sincerely hoping he hadn't signed them on for more than they could handle. Adele and Frank had jumped at the chance when they'd talked about it, but the reality might be more than they had thought. Yet one more thing to worry about. They'd never done more than have the actual wedding day on the grounds and then host the couple on their wedding night, along with perhaps some other relatives. This providing of huge meals was new, since the wedding party usually brought in caterers.

He scooped mashed potatoes into china bowls and poured gravy into three boats. Seventeen hungry people had come for lunch, and it was going to be the best lunch they'd ever had. Fortunately, he'd thought ahead enough to hire a few extras to help.

"I'm going out." Adele hefted a tray heavily laden with plates of everything anyone could possibly want for a Thanksgiving dinner in August.

"Right behind you." He picked up his own tray. Chelsea chose that moment to burst through the swinging door, nearly knocking down Adele in the process.

"Oh, my gosh, I'm so sorry! Are you okay, Adele?"

Being the professional at all times, Adele simply smiled at Chelsea. "I didn't drop a single thing. I call that impressive, not just okay." And she swept out.

Trouble brewed in Chelsea's amber eyes. Before

she asked, he placed his tray on the butcher block and led her into the small office Frank used occasionally. "What's going on?"

Glancing over her shoulder to the closed door, she leaned into him. That lemon scent floated to him, filling his senses in a way the fragrant kitchen had not.

"I made a mistake and I don't know how to get out of it."

She had always taken her problems to Paige when they were younger. He'd be in the front seat driving them somewhere and couldn't help but overhear every crush, every heartbreak. He'd normally tried to stay out of it, but every once in a while he'd cut in with the male perspective. She'd bring her problems to Paige and vice versa. Solutions were reached in grassy fields or at the diner over root beer floats. He didn't have any root beer and he wasn't Paige, but he'd do his best. "I'm sure whatever it is we can take care of it. Does it have to be done now? I have to get the food out to the table before lunch is served."

She bit her lip, plumping it up on the right side. Temptation ran through him, thick and hot. Cupping her chin, he leaned forward, but she dropped her head leaving him to place a soft kiss on the crown of her hair.

He lifted her face until she met his eyes again. "What's up, buttercup?"

She smiled, but the smile was overshadowed by her tearing eyes. "This is going to be a whole lot more than I had thought, and I don't know how far you're willing to go."

Telling her "all the way" would not take that sheen out of her eyes. "It's not that big of a deal, Chelsea. It's only a week, right? Besides, you and Mazzy are the only two guests I have this week, so I would be sitting idle if you weren't here, anyway. I can play doting suitor at a few of the get-togethers. What are old friend's big brothers for?"

She threw her arms around his neck and pulled him close. Just as he was mapping out the feel of her against him, she pulled back. Her eyes were still misty, but the smile was stronger. "I totally should have told my mother I was engaged to some guy back in Bettleton to avoid all this, but I didn't think fast enough on my feet. I'm going to owe you at the end of the week, if we survive. Thanks for being such a good sport, Jack."

She wiped under her eyes and took a quick glance in the mirror hanging on the wall before heading back out into the kitchen. He heard her thank Frank for everything and then the swinging door whooshed shut. The tray could wait a few more seconds while he found his smile for the rest of the guests. Yeah, he was a good sport, but was he going to lose a piece of himself when Chelsea walked away? That remained to be seen.

****

Lunch went off without a hitch. Jack had played his part well, coming in to wrap his arm around her every once in a while or kissing the top of her head when he walked past. Nothing overt, but those kisses and touches had set something on fire inside her. She'd just have to extinguish that fire, to have any hope of living through the next few days.

Now everything was quiet in the big house. Mazzy had gone down for bed without much of a fight about forty minutes ago. Spending time with her grandparents was going to make the child spoiled, but Chelsea couldn't make herself put her foot down. Normally they only saw Leigh and Hugh a couple of times a year, when her parents could get down to Bettleton. They talked often on the phone, yet it wasn't the same.

Taking the baby monitor with her, Chelsea descended the stairs. She wanted a book to read in bed. She'd mistakenly assumed she'd be so busy she'd fall exhausted into bed every night; however, so much was already laid out in the lists from Paige that she had a free night.

Those free moments were going to be precious as the wedding lead-up really got into swing tomorrow, so she might as well take advantage now. She could seek out Jack, but she didn't want to intrude more than she already had. She wished she had never said anything to her mom about an engagement.

And yet there was a part of her that enjoyed having a man's attention for the first time in a long while. That kind of thinking was not going to do her any good, though.

In the library, she went straight to the bookshelves filled with paperbacks.

"Did Mazzy go down okay?" Jack said from behind her.

She hadn't seen him sitting in the chair facing the unlit fireplace. With her hand on her heart to calm its racing, she cleared her throat.

"Um, yes, she went down just fine, thanks. I think today has been a big day, and we have a whole lot more in front of us. I'm going to have to make sure she gets a daily nap if I don't want her to be grumpy." She was rambling but couldn't seem to stop herself. Jack had stood up, looking relaxed and casual in a way that made her feel anything but casual or relaxed.

Low-slung jeans sat on his slim hips, a dark green T-shirt fit him to perfection and ended only inches below the waist of the jeans. His dark hair was slightly tousled and his green eyes sparkled in the low light of the library.

"I think she's going to do fine. She's a tough little girl and quite the comedian." A slight curve in his lips told her he found her daughter a pleasure instead of the burden Paul had considered her.

"Well, thanks," she said into the slight pause. "I guess I should go on upstairs. I'm not going to be the most pleasant of people, either, if I don't get proper rest."

As she went past him, he made a grab for her hand. She let him catch it, anticipating the way his palm would feel against hers. They'd been good friends once, and he'd held her hand on numerous occasions when they'd gone hiking or to help her out of a car when she and Paige needed to be driven around. He was a toucher. She hadn't appreciated that quality enough until it was totally absent with Paul.

This thinking about her ex-husband had to stop. It was completely inappropriate to the situation. Paul and Jack had nothing in common and didn't need to. Chelsea was not looking for another long-term commitment; she just needed him to play his part until Sunday.

"Hey, do you have a few moments before you head up?" Jack played with her fingers, touching each of the pads in a rhythm only he was privy to.

"Um, sure." Perhaps they should take some time to discuss what their story was and how they were going to play those parts.

"Good. Meet me in the speakeasy in three minutes. I have to run up to my rooms for something. I'll be right back. You know where everything is down there." He loped out of the room, a tall, lean man with a backside she should not be staring at.

As she walked down the stairs to what normally would be a basement in any other house, she lectured herself. She would not let Jack be a rebound crush. For one thing, he was better than that, and for another, there was no hope there. She wouldn't be moving back and he wouldn't be moving to her. He liked her kid, sure, but that did not make any difference in the scheme of things.

Three minutes on the dot later, Jack bounded back down the stairs. Chelsea sat in one of the high-backed pub booths with her tightly clenched hands in her lap. How to start the conversation? It wasn't as if she'd ever done anything like this before, so she didn't know the rules. She'd read plenty of romance novels where the fake engagement turned into something more, but she wasn't a heroine in a book and this was not going to end happily.

Clinking sounded behind her, and then there was Jack with two glasses of wine and a smile that made her wonder why no one had yet snapped up the town's most eligible bachelor.

"I think we need to set some ground rules," she blurted out.

"Yeah, I was thinking the same thing. But first," he nudged her glass toward her, "try this new wine I'm thinking about carrying. The winery is right over the next mountain. I was thinking it'd be nice to support someone local."

She took a sip, rolled the fruity liquid around her tongue, and relaxed, something she hadn't done in a long time. Though this conversation might not be terribly comfortable, she was sitting across from a man who had come to her rescue more times than she had thought, once she'd had time to run back over their years together. Of course Paige had always been there, but she'd realized Jack was in far more of her memories than she had anticipated.

That counted for something in her book. And while she didn't relish the thought of using him, she didn't think it was exactly like that.

"Very nice. I bet this will be a great addition to the speakeasy."

"I'm glad you think so. It's also the wine we'll be serving at the wedding on Saturday."

Which brought her right back to the point she'd been about to make before he distracted her. "Look, I think we need to get some sort of story ironed out, figure out the boundaries of what we're going to do until after the wedding." Something occurred to her and she gasped. "I didn't even ask if you were dating someone. Oh, my, this isn't going to get you in trouble with another woman, is it?" Her face was on fire with embarrassment. Thank God for the low lighting in the room.

He chuckled. "No, you're not going to get me in trouble with another woman. There aren't any in my life right now, so no worries."

"Thank goodness."

He peered at her over the rim of his wine glass. "What would you have done if I had a girlfriend?"

"I have no idea. Talk about awkward, though. My mom would have known right away I was lying."

"Instead, you're going to just lie to her for the week, then break up with me, and she'll be none the wiser?" His eyes twinkled, but there was something more behind his words.

"When you put it like that, it sounds mercenary." She plopped her chin into her hand, rimming her glass with her pointer finger. "I don't like lying to her, and believe me when I say this is not exactly comfortable for me. But I just can't face a room full of bachelors at a wedding. And I know for certain she wouldn't just confine it to the wedding. Various single men would show up at every function this week, from the barbecue to the rehearsal dinner. Heck, she'd probably have some guy accidentally bump into us while we were having facials. I just don't want that kind of pressure while I'm here on vacation."

"So you'd rather pretend to be my fiancé?"

His words made her take a second look at him. "Is this going to be really tough for you? We lost touch over the years, of course, but if you don't think you can pull it off, I'll figure something else out."

He touched her hand, just the back of it, with a fingertip. "Don't worry about it, Chelsea. I'm sure it won't be a problem. And it's only a week, right?"

"Right." She gulped her wine as he continued touching her. She shouldn't feel anything, with so little of their bodies touching, but there it was. That tingle from the point of contact all the way up to her brain. And since she had yet to finish her first glass of wine, there was no way it was the alcohol.

"Ground rules," she blurted out before she could

turn her hand over to clutch his fingers.

"Ground rules." He slouched against the tall booth back. "Well, since I've never done anything like this before, I don't have much to offer as far as ground rules go."

"It's not like I've ever done this before, either."

"I wasn't saying you had, so let's just agree this is blind territory for both of us." He rubbed his chin. "Is there anything I should know about your life now that's different from before?"

"Like what?"

"Do you like broccoli now? Did you end up finishing college? Do you sleep in the nude?"

She leaned forward in her seat to swat him for that last one. "I don't think you need to know about my sleeping habits. Let's see. We could have fallen in love by email and talking on the phone. Since we've known each other forever, it's not a sudden thing so much as just seeing each other in a different light."

"True."

"So we're getting married because we know we want to be together forever, but we're going to have a long engagement and continue to get to know each other as full-fledged adults instead of all those days together as kids."

"Sounds good to me."

"I'm still going home after the wedding to tie things up, but I'm going to be coming back after I quit my job, to find something up here."

"Okay."

"Aren't you going to help at all?" She blew a breath out, ruffling her bangs.

"Sorry," he said with a smile. "I think you should

change the part about finding something up here, though. Don't you think most people will assume you're going to help me with the inn? Plus, jobs of your caliber are in short supply in this area."

"I hadn't thought about that."

"See, I helped."

She swatted him again, and this time he caught her hand.

"I brought something down for you. I hope it fits, because I'm not sure about getting it refitted."

He placed a beautiful emerald set in a ring of diamonds on her left ring finger. Her breath caught as she stuck her hand out in front of her, turning it left and right. It was the most stunning ring she had ever seen. And it fit perfectly.

"Where did you get this on such short notice? Were you engaged before?"

"Nah, it was my grandmother's engagement ring." He took a healthy swig of his own wine.

****

The ring fit as if it had been made for her. Jack fought back the sigh rising in his chest. Of course it did. Could fate have been any crueler to him? He wouldn't deny there had been a part of him who'd had fantasies about Chelsea coming up here, falling in love with the area all over again, and the two of them getting to know each other as more than teenagers. Maybe she would have taken his calls and gone out with him a few times when she came back for visits. And that was him settling in a way he hadn't settled before now.

"Okay, so the ring's out of the way. I think we have the story straight. Now what should I expect this week?" he said, reminding himself this was temporary.

The first time he'd been engaged and it wouldn't last more than a week, with him being dumped at the end. Great.

She continued to look at the emerald his grandmother had worn for all fifty-seven years of her marriage. Shifting it back and forth on her hand brought light and heat to a stone he had always thought of as cold, or utilitarian at the least. On her it could have been the sun.

"Well, I imagine my mom is probably going to pull for you to be at most of the family stuff, but I can make excuses, if you want. You do have a business to run, and she can't expect you to be at every function." Her amber eyes glowed in the soft candlelight of the wall sconce.

"I can probably make most of them." He shrugged. "I already know your family, so it's not as if I'm going to be uncomfortable."

"No, you're just going to be playing a part. If it means anything, I told my mom to keep it to herself, so I'll only have my family to tell about the break-up, if that's any consolation."

"No big deal. But we might want to come up with some big romantic way that I proposed. I don't think your mom is going to go with me just handing you the ring over the table."

"You proposed out in the gazebo where Belinda is going to get married. It was a moonlit night, my first night here, and you didn't want another minute to go by without asking me on bended knee to make a forever life with you."

She painted a picture he could see in his head. The way the trailing moonflowers would have highlighted her hair, even muted in the near dark, the way the tiny sparkle lights would have twinkled, twined around the white wood structure, and glowed against her creamy skin. The moonlight would have reflected in her amber eyes, lighting them up when he presented her with the ring. The words would have flowed from his mouth in his nervousness.

He cut himself off before he could go further. This was unnecessary torture. It also wouldn't change their circumstances or make the vision any less false.

"Sounds great." He raised his glass. "To our one-week engagement."

She clinked her glass to his. What should have been a bright noise rang hollow.

Chapter Five

"Bye, Mommy, bye!" Mazzy waved furiously at Chelsea from her position in the front foyer of the inn Tuesday morning. As she did, she took a step closer to Jack's side. Chelsea was leaving Mazzy here with Leigh for a few hours while she ran errands. He looked forward to more of the little girl's antics, but was not especially ready to be grilled by Leigh.

"Have a good day, sweetheart." Chelsea bent down to place a kiss on each of the girl's cheeks and then one on her nose.

"You, too, Mommy." With her words, she took another step toward him.

Chelsea walked backwards in the direction of the door, waving, each curve moving in enticing ways he should not be noticing. With each wave, Mazzy inched another fraction of a step toward him.

Because of her tiny feet it took a little while, but eventually she was up against his leg and grinning at him like the Cheshire cat the moment her mother closed the door.

Bouncing one finger off his knee, then two, then one again, she suddenly turned shy, looking at her shiny black shoes. "So, Big Man, you want to play Candyland with me today?" When she gestured for him to come closer, he bent at the waist, unable to resist the magic of this little girl. "Grammy is not so good at losing, and I don't want her to have to cheat," she whispered in a loud voice.

He had a ton of things to do today. And yet Leigh wouldn't talk about the engagement in front of Mazzy until Chelsea gave her the okay. It was the perfect solution. Plus, his business hinged on accommodating his guests.

Or at least that was the excuse he allowed himself to believe while he went to find the old board game in the attic. He handed his list to Adele as he passed her in the third floor hallway.

****

Three hours later, Chelsea had a fifth of her list done and some artful highlights in her brown hair. Feeling good, she walked into the parlor to find her daughter sound asleep on the floor, swaddled in her blanket, with her favorite teddy under her arm.

Mazzy's other hand rested on the gingerbread man in her favorite game. At some point she must have moved her arm and swept the cards from the pile into a rainbow of moves across the multicolored board. Chelsea took a moment to just enjoy the sight of her little tornado at a standstill.

Looking around the room for her mother, she was instead hit by the sight of the very attractive Jack Barton sprawled in the big wing-backed chair near the fireplace. His normally neat hair was standing up on end, his long arms draped over the arms of the chair, his long legs thrust out in front of him. He, too, was out like a light. She couldn't imagine this was his normal routine. Mazzy must have worn him out at some point.

Silently snickering, she backed out of the room, pulling the door closed, then went in search of her mother, who should have been watching her daughter. She found the other woman in the kitchen. No surprise there.

"So anyway, Frank, the mashed potatoes were divine yesterday afternoon, but have you thought of adding a hint of rosemary to the mix? It flavors the potatoes just right and makes the whole thing pop."

Frank stood at the stove, using a spoon to stir the big pot on the range top, nodding at her mom and smiling. Leave it to her mom to find the kitchen and start trying to run it. Mazzy's monitor stood right next to her on the counter she leaned against.

"Why doesn't it surprise me to find you here?" Chelsea stood in the doorway to the kitchen, resting a hip against the doorjamb to keep the swinging door open.

"Oh, come in, hon. Frank and I were just discussing the merits of herbs."

"Really? Or were you just telling Frank how to make a wonderful dish more like you would have."

Her mother laughed and blushed. "You caught me."

"I always appreciate talking food with someone, Leigh, so you don't worry about trying to help me out. Jack always tells me to spice things up a bit, so I value your opinion." Frank set down his spoon on a cradle Chelsea would have sworn was a mermaid without a top on—fully anatomically correct.

Chelsea cleared her throat. "So how long ago did Mazzy go down, and how many games of Candyland did she talk Jack into playing with her?"

"Oh, that! They had a blast. Mazzy tromped him about ten times in two hours. I kept trying to play, too, but Mazzy had her mind set on Mr. Big Man and wanted nothing to do with me. Jack agreed to her demands to play." Her mom waved a hand in the air as if signaling it was all well and good.

And then she winked as if they had a secret, which they did.

Chelsea swallowed, hoping Jack hadn't minded babysitting when her mother should have been watching Mazzy. A fake engagement was one thing, but she hadn't thought of her mom allowing Jack and Mazzy to bond. Her heart was probably in the right place, wanting her granddaughter to get comfortable with the man her daughter was going to marry. But she didn't know the whole truth, and this was just one more thing that could bite Chelsea in the inevitable end.

"Oh. My. Don't you look glamorous? Doesn't she look glamorous, Frank?" Chelsea's face was in her mother's hand a second later and the older woman turned her head to get the full effect of the more flattering cut done by the lady at Damsel in Distress.

Chelsea had styled her hair in the easiest and most maintenance-free way possible for years now. Being a secretary, she needed to look professional as she greeted clients, but she did not need to be the height of fashion. So she wasn't. Now she felt the fringe around her face, the long bangs sweeping over her forehead, and hoped it looked as nice as her mother thought.

"You look like a million bucks, chicky," Frank said with a wink.

"Um, thanks." A muffled snort came over the monitor. The noise meant Mazzy was about to wake up. "I should go. Mazzy and I have to get ready for dinner at your house."

"I hope you're bringing Jack with you, dear." The narrowing of her mother's eyes warned Chelsea, but she'd never been one for heeding warnings.

"Um, we haven't had much of a chance to talk about it. But I'll ask him."

"I can get Mazzy ready then, so you have some time. This is your vacation, too."

"That's okay; I want some Mazzy hugs and stories." She trotted out of the kitchen before her mother could stop her. But not before she heard her mother lamenting that Chelsea never took a break, hardly ever let anyone help her.

Shaking her head, Chelsea tiptoed back into the parlor, not wanting to wake Jack. Instead, she found him moving her little one to the plush couch in the far corner. That must have been the snort, but Mazzy had fallen back to sleep in Jack's strong arms.

Chelsea waited for him to put the little girl on the couch, then watched as he tucked her blanket back around her, making sure her teddy bear was right next to her face. A little piece of her melted at the sight, but she firmed it right back up without the slightest pause.

When he turned around, he smiled at her, a crooked smile that crinkled the edges of his incredible eyes. Chelsea leaned against the archway separating the parlor from the next room. She needed to shore herself up this time.

On nearly silent feet, Jack walked over to her. Her heart did a ridiculous little flutter dance without her permission when he touched her arm lightly.

"She is one tough customer when it comes to that game. You must have taught her well, or her dad did."

It was an opening she should resist. She had told

him some of the details of her life that first night, more
than she had told anyone. But this was digging into the
day-to-day aspect of Paul's neglect and disinterest, not
just the overall picture. And yet this was her friend
Jack, and she hadn't been able to open up to anyone.

"Her dad never had time to teach her anything. My
own dad is the one who taught her every dirty move she
knows in Candyland. They play whenever my parents
come down for a visit." She had tried to lighten her first
statement, but the way he was peering at her as if
looking into her heart made it flutter all over again.

No, no, no! She had not been attracted to anyone in
a long time. Even before Mazzy was born, she and Paul
hadn't slept together in months. But they had stuck it
out for the baby, until he walked away. It was
completely not fair that for the first time in a long time
she felt herself drawn in. And to someone who was
dutifully posing as her fiancé because they'd been
friends years ago.

****

Well that was certainly an interesting piece of
information, Jack thought, trying out in his head the
concept of being able to walk away from that cutely
snoozing little angel on the couch. To never play a
game with her or teach her anything. To lose out on the
chance to mold your own child.

He couldn't help but look at Mazzy for just a brief
second before he zeroed back in on Chelsea. How could
you walk away from a child? A marriage was one thing,
as he knew from various friends. But this was a small
person whom you had created and who loved you
without reservations or expectations except that you
would love her back. What kind of person did it take to

walk away from all this?

And what did you say to someone who had just revealed this hurt? He hadn't been told much about her relationship beyond what she had shared that first night. It was only since the wedding planning began that he had talked much with her family. Apparently this was more than he would have heard from the grapevine. The whole thing had been kept pretty mum, and now he might know why.

He tried but felt lame when he said, "I'm sorry. Obviously, it's his loss."

She made a noncommittal noise and looked away over her lovely shoulder. He could take a hint without being beaten over the head with it.

Subject-change time.

"So did you need anything?"

That brought her smile back and her gaze back to his. "Thanks for not belaboring the leaving-man thing."

Her honesty and openness were two of the things he had liked about her all those years ago. She cut right to the point without any dancing around it. Her lush body was worth liking, too, but that thought would not help him at this time.

"I won't say another word about it if you don't bring it up. Well, just one more thing, and then that's it. He's missing out on seeing a very strong-minded and wonderful little person grow right before his eyes."

"Strong-minded is right, and I can tell you she mostly gets that from my side of the family."

He couldn't deny the truth of that statement after dealing with her sister and her mother lately, and her, years ago. "But it will serve her well in life, so it can't be a bad thing."

"I won't say it's a bad thing, but it can be a flaw if not tempered." She smiled ruefully and plucked at the sleeve of her fitted shirt.

He had a feeling she was talking about more than just Mazzy, but he let it go. He'd said his piece and didn't need to go further on the subject, which was obviously still painful to her.

Though he had to admit, if just to himself, that she intrigued him.

He'd like to know what kind of trouble her strong-mindedness had gotten her into since they were young. If he were being honest, he wanted to know everything about her since she had left, no matter how small. That way led to danger, though, and he was not in a position to have danger in his life.

Back to that subject change. "So any favors?"

"Actually, there is one thing you can do for me, if you don't mind. I'd like to set up a surprise, but I need your help." She pocketed the monitoring device for Mazzy, gave the child one last kiss on the cheek, and walked out of the room.

"I am at your service," he said, following along behind and mentally preparing himself for nearly anything.

"Tonight's the first dinner at my parents' house. I know you said you could only come to some of the activities, so I understand if this isn't one of them, but my mom is in there yakking Frank's ear off and asked me to bring you tonight. Will that be okay?"

"Absolutely. I'll bring wine, and we can drive over together. Will that suit the situation?"

"Yes, and thanks. For everything." With that she leaned up and kissed him on the cheek. It was all he could do not to grab her and show her what a real kiss could be like between them.

His eyes followed her path as she left, and then he called one of his best friends from college. He was in way over his head, and his man Dex could talk some sense into him. He was a lawyer, knew all the ins and outs of the stupid things people did, and could give him the reality check he needed.

He took the steps two at a time to get up to his suite of rooms for some privacy. Dex, thankfully, answered on the third ring.

"Hey, isn't this the big week? Did someone already cause property damage and you're wondering how you might go about suing them for everything they have?"

"Yes, it is. No, they haven't, and I'm not." He blew out a gust of air. He felt like such a girl for calling his friend for advice, but there was no one else he could really talk to, and he needed that dose of reality.

"What can I do for you then? Do you actually have a rare night off and want to go shoot some hoops?"

"No, not that either, but it sure would be a lot easier if it was that simple."

"What has occurred, and what can I do to resolve the issue?" Dexter Zegray, attorney at law, turned serious and quiet, his voice notching up to that highfalutin place he went when he thought there was a problem to solve.

"I'm fake-engaged to someone I remember but barely know, and now I have to pretend to be the doting fiancé for the next week even though it might just kill me."

Dex laughed, and Jack could imagine him throwing his head back and slapping the arm of his leather chair in his office. "Oh, man, what the hell have you done?"

"Put myself in a position I don't know if I can handle."

"Sounds like it. So you don't need legal advice, you need heart advice? Should we paint each other's nails and play dreamy music while we're at it?"

"Jesus, man, you're making me sound like a sissy."

"No, sorry. Do you at least like the lady, or is she really a bad seed?"

"Unfortunately, she's perfect and that's part of the problem."

"How so?"

"She's Paige's oldest friend."

"Oldest as in pushing ninety?"

That made the tension in Jack's shoulders break and laughter spill out. "God, no. Oldest as in they've been together since they were five."

"Is this the one you used to cart around with Paige?"

"Yes. Chelsea Moore." Jack picked up the few things in his room that were out of place, just to give himself something to do.

"So let me get this straight. You have a girl in your house that you actually like, after being what amounts to a monk, and you're pseudo-engaged to her. You see this as a problem how?"

"When you put it that way, it seems more of a problem than even I was thinking."

"Seriously? Why? Do you really think Paige is going to have a hissy fit if she finds out about it? Maybe she'll be really happy."

"And that would be even worse. I've never been engaged. This is one that could rock all our family and friends, and when we break up they'll take her side because it couldn't possibly be her fault. I'm the guy, and therefore I'll be the dog."

"You are way over-thinking this. I would give just about anything to get Zoe Bradley to pay attention to me, and she acts like I have the plague. If I could waltz her into a fake engagement and make it real, I'd do it in a heartbeat."

Jack shook his head even though Dex couldn't see it. He knew the girls down at Decadence, and he didn't know what had Dex latching onto Zoe. She was an attractive woman and interesting to be around. In fact all of them—May, Claudia, and Zoe—were lookers with great personalities. But Jack had always envisioned himself with someone a little more low key, someone who would be a partner, someone he could share things with. Not that any of them couldn't be shared with. May and her husband Brad were very happy, from what he'd seen, and expecting their first child. Claudia and her best friend Nate had just gotten together, after being friends for a long, long time and Nate essentially raising her child with her without the benefits of a relationship. But he'd never looked at any of them as anything more than business women who were at the top of their game.

Dex had a soft spot and a hot streak for Zoe. Jack didn't know why he hadn't gotten her to go out with him just yet, but he must be lying in wait to see what she'd do next.

"So I guess you don't have any words of wisdom for me as far as this totally unorthodox situation, then?"

"I say enjoy the ride, my man, and get the T-shirt when you're done. There's nothing wrong with doing something other than working for once." He paused and Jack heard something like pages being turned. "Hey, speaking of that. Will you be able to fit in a game of darts this week? Or is this Chelsea girl going to take up all your time?"

"Let me see what I can do. I have to go to all these family function things now, since supposedly I'm an engaged man, so we'll probably have to do it after."

"Buck up, Jack. Maybe there will be some side benefits for you that will make it all worth your while."

They hung up, but all Jack could think of was the one side benefit that would be more than just on the side. He was trying to fight the urge, but there was something inside him that was calling out for Chelsea to be the one even if they had only recently reconnected. He'd enjoyed everything about their email conversations. They'd talked about inconsequential things after the first few conversations. She asked how his day was and he did the same. She asked his opinion about an issue at her job—once it was how to handle a confrontational employee—and he gave her the benefit of his experience before he'd settled down with the inn. It was almost like they were building a bridge, one he'd just realized he wanted to run across.

But there was still the fact that she did not live here and he would not, could not, leave the area. Even if he fell in love with her, which he doubted he'd do in a week's time, there was no way they could be together.

And that solidified for him the fact that the engagement had to stay fake and he wouldn't pursue anything more than what she wanted to give. And she'd leave at the end and he'd be fine.

****

The show began at her parents' house. Chelsea couldn't think about the whole situation any other way. She was playing a part and so was Jack. She only hoped no one said anything overt when it came to Mazzy. Jack was all she talked about the whole time while they freshened up in their room. Jack played with her. Jack tickled her. Jack was a good sport about losing, unlike Grammy. He talked Frank into giving them graham crackers and milk and letting them eat in the library. He'd read her a story and gone to get her stuffed bear when she'd asked.

The gestures were small, but to a young girl who had biannual visits from her grandparents and no male role model, they had taken on brilliant proportions. It was heartbreaking to hear how impressed Mazzy was with so little, when such things should have been an everyday life occurrence.

She, Jack, and Mazzy arrived right on time at the large colonial house where Chelsea had grown up. Flowers of every shade and shape bedded down in front of the covered porch decked out with rocking chairs and swagged flags left over from July Fourth. The late afternoon sun lit up the stained glass of the upstairs windows.

"Grammy can't wait to see me," Mazzy sang, gripping Jack's hand and Chelsea's. She'd already asked for three swings between the two of them in the ten steps from the car, but with the way her child had glowed after playing a couple of board games this afternoon, Chelsea gave in every time.

The front door swung open before they had crossed the beautifully weathered porch. Her dad stood in the doorway with a smile on his craggy face and his arms open wide.

Mazzy dropped both their hands to skip up to Pop-Pop. Kissing the soft hair at her crown, he hugged her to him, just like he used to with Chelsea. He put her down and told her where the candy was, and she was off like a shot.

"You shouldn't do that." Chelsea said. "Mom is not going to be happy if Mazzy ruins her appetite."

"Nonsense, my girl." He dragged her into a hug, his big embrace consuming her. She wanted to stay here forever.

But then he let her go to shake Jack's hand. "Good to see you, son." He winked. "I hear that might be more than just wishful thinking before long."

"Dad," Chelsea hissed, looking over his shoulder to make sure Mazzy wasn't within hearing distance. "We haven't told her yet."

"Well, at least let me see the rock your mom says knocked her socks right off her sneakered feet."

Chelsea turned the ring around from her palm and stuck her hand out to let her father take it, then fought to not snatch it back. As a precaution against too many stares or awkward questions from her daughter, she'd kept it on the correct finger but facing the wrong direction until someone asked to see it. She deliberately hadn't looked at that hand two dozen times since last night. She hadn't been as stalwart the other two hundred times. When she had dreamed of getting married one day, long ago, this would have been the ring she would have imagined with her heart even if she hadn't known the design with her head. The emerald was flawless and looked just right nestled in the cluster of diamonds. It was the "something old" that could be turned into something new. A new promise to fulfill after the love of the first one, made with the same ring, had gone beyond the grave.

And here she was getting fanciful when she should have been listening to her dad, or at least saving Jack from the myriad questions Hugh Moore was throwing out. She loved the ring, but that didn't mean she wasn't going to give it back when it was all said and done.

This was only temporary, which included the ring that could have been made just for her.

They shuffled into the crowd and made the rounds. She was surprised to see all the women from Decadence here, but she shouldn't have been. After the way her mother had acted in the dress shop, cooing over every line and detail of Belinda's beautiful dress, it made sense that her mom would have invited them.

She met Brad, who was May's husband, and Nate, who was with Claudia but not yet married to her. Mazzy immediately broke away from Grammylove when she saw Justin playing one of the old-time pinball machines her dad had set up in the billiard room. Chelsea had spent many an hour there, when she wasn't traipsing around with Paige, and could remember Jack hitting the high score a number of times.

For a brief moment, Chelsea hoped like hell that no one had told the elder Bartons that she and Jack were engaged. She did not want to be seen as the one who had broken their son's heart. Not that she would have, really, but some continued acting would be necessary. Maybe she wouldn't be coming home as often if she had to pretend to be broken up with Jack every time she visited.

She grabbed a glass of champagne and downed it.

Liquid courage was not going to help, but she wasn't turning it down, either.

"So where's the bride?" Jack whispered in her ear.

"I'm not sure. She was supposed to be here five minutes ago, but you know how she can be."

"No doubt. In fact I told her the wedding was a half hour before it actually is, per Paige's instructions, just so you know."

Her laughter was spontaneous and turned several heads in the immediate vicinity. She dipped her chin and put her mouth on her glass of champagne. "You're bad," she mumbled.

"No, I'm very, very good." He drifted a hand over her shoulder, sifting through the new shorter strands at her neck. She couldn't suppress the shiver but supposed it made for a good show to the people who were still looking and smiling at the two of them.

"Why don't you go see what's going on with your mom, and I'll keep an eye on the kid. I think she's trying to get Justin to beat my high score, and we can't have that." He kissed the spot where his hand had rested, right at the nape of her neck, and there was no suppressing this shiver either. God, he did things to her, and he shouldn't.

Fortunately Belinda chose that moment to make her big entrance, and there were rounds of hugs and hellos to participate in. She ducked out to the kitchen to see if she could help and make sure that everything was in place in her capacity of wedding coordinator.

Her mom, of course, had everything in complete order and lined up like a surgeon. Tiny curls of vegetables in Belinda's wedding colors garnished meat and cheese platters. An array of dips were set up in bread bowls, with the hollowed-out parts of the bread in piles to be used for dipping. A huge sheet cake sat on the small breakfast nook table waiting for Belinda and Marcus to practice their cake-cutting moves.

"It looks perfect, Mom."

"Thanks, sweetie. And just think, this is perfect practice for yours in a little bit. I do need the actual date as soon as you have it, because I think it would be great to get together with Jack's mom to see what kind of ideas she has for the many parties I'm sure we'll have. They have a lot of out-of-town relatives, so they'll need ample time to get here. And I really want to do right by you this time, since I wasn't able to do more than take you out to lunch after the last one."

Chelsea's gut clenched at the reminder of her wedding day with Paul. It had been a quickie thing, done at the justice of the peace, with a small lunch afterward—at Denny's, if she remembered right. She'd thought she was so in love she didn't need the trappings. She'd even worn a little sundress that she'd picked up at a thrift store. It wasn't much, and she still believed that with the right person it could have been beautiful, but even then she'd had her misgivings about her decision. He'd been attentive and loving but totally focused on what he wanted. As far as he'd been concerned, there was no need for family or friends because they were already pretty much married. She'd gone along with it because at the time she'd thought it was romantic, but later she'd known better.

And then it had ended much more quietly than it had started, with even less fanfare than a short wedding with lunch. He hadn't even taken her to dinner. He'd simply told her he was moving out and would have his things out by the weekend. And he had. She hadn't seen him since. She'd tried to call and email, but he'd shut down his phone and ignored her emails except to tell her once that he'd pay child support. The divorce was signed without contest, and they'd really had nothing to split. She hadn't wanted anything but for him to love them, and if she couldn't have that, she didn't want anything more.

Maybe Mazzy was better off without him.

But even now that felt disloyal. Shouldn't she continue to try to get him involved? Wouldn't Mazzy miss not having a father, especially when the man lived less than ten minutes from their apartment?

She crunched her way through a carrot, absentmindedly, until her mother took her left hand.

"Holy wow! That is beautiful, sweetheart! Where on earth did he find something that is so you?"

It was just the two of them in the kitchen. Chelsea was tempted to just break down and tell her mother it was all a farce. But she couldn't. It was only a few more days, and then she'd come up with some spectacular reason why it wouldn't work out between her and Jack. She could pull it off until Sunday. She had to. And then she'd call her mother and tell her it just wasn't a good fit for either of them, and it would be forgotten in a short time. Or at least that was what she'd started telling herself, to put down her guilt for the lying.

"It was his grandmother's ring."

"Oh, my word, that's lovely. You never did tell me where he proposed," she said as she retrieved pigs-in-a-blanket from the oven and popped some tiny quiches in.

Thank God they'd worked this out in the

speakeasy. "Actually it was the first night I got here. He took me out to the gazebo, where Belinda's getting married, and got down on one knee, with the moonlight shining and the smell of flowers fresh in the air. He told me he loved me and wanted me to know the kind of commitment he wanted to make to me. He asked me to be his and to wear his ring."

Her mom had a tear in her eye and swiped at the ones trickling down her cheek. She came in for a full body hug. "Oh, honey, I am so very happy for you. I wasn't sure if you would ever find anyone who was worthy, but you have, and that just makes my heart sing!"

It made the bottom of Chelsea's stomach drop out. She could almost see Jack doing that, looking at her with those incredible eyes, his deep voice giving her the words she'd never thought she wanted again.

It would have been perfect if it were true. But it wasn't true, and she had to remember that. They'd be breaking up in a matter of days. Her mother was going to be heartbroken. Her father said it would be more than wishful thinking to call Jack "son," and she'd crash that right to the ground.

She had opened her mouth to tell her mother it was all a lie when Belinda came hustling into the kitchen. "Hey, Chelsea. Everything looks great! Do we have all the food I listed for Paige?"

"Yes." She tucked her hand behind her back.

"Oh, wait. I know that gesture. Did he give you one? Tell me he did! Let's see this ring."

Chelsea obliged by giving her hand over.

"Wow, that is amazing. I can just see all the colors you could build around this gem to make the perfect wedding. Oh! Something at Christmas, with garlands and sleek red velvet dresses. It could be outside for the vows, with red capes trimmed in white fur with fur muffs. I'll get with Paige to discuss it!" And she started rummaging around in the junk drawer, presumably for pen and paper. She chortled when she found them and started writing furiously while their mother looked on fondly.

This was a hole Chelsea was never going to be able to dig herself out of.

****

Driving home with Mazzy snoring softly in the back seat and Chelsea looking out the side window at the abundance of stars in the sky, Jack congratulated himself on a job well done. He'd made the appropriate noises, held Chelsea's hand when it felt right, and stroked his hand over her hair every once in a while when he walked past her. For anyone who had been looking, they were a couple in love, ready to make a commitment to each other sometime in the next year. Someone had questioned Chelsea about what she would do when she moved up here, and Chelsea had evaded the question by saying she would look into things when the details were finalized.

Good answer, but it made him yearn for things that just weren't real.

Pulling up in front of the house, he gently shook Chelsea out of her reverie, then hooked his arms under the little girl who had stolen his heart long before she'd snuggled into his lap to fall asleep after running around like a kid with way too much sugar—which she had been.

He had to be careful, he reminded himself for the

hundredth time as he climbed up the stairs to Mazzy and Chelsea's room. He could get way too used to this. He just didn't know if his heart could take it. Fake engagement or not, it felt too real. He should never have agreed to fake something that fulfilled the dreams he hadn't known were buried inside himself.

Chapter Six

"I need a change in the menu for the reception." Belinda Moore, soon to be Belinda Rushland, swept into the foyer with her usual flair on Wednesday morning. Her face set in rigid lines, the morning sunshine streaming across her back, she could have been an avenging angel, but she had nothing to avenge —other than every little detail of the upcoming event, Jack mused resignedly.

Three days remained until the wedding, and Jack had thought things were moving along nicely, even if Chelsea had been avoiding him since last night. It was probably for the best, since all he'd dreamed about last night was kissing her for real. It had haunted his dreams. But now he had this woman ghosting him with her demands. Honestly, he didn't know if he'd be able to survive another request.

The inn was hosting another breakfast this morning, this one for just the bridal party so details could be finalized. Quiche, fruit, and orange juice were to be on the table in twenty minutes when everyone showed up for the meal, but Belinda had been here and hounding him intermittently over the past forty-five minutes. He hadn't heard Chelsea or Mazzy stir from upstairs yet, but he desperately wished they would.

Jack barely resisted putting his head into his hands. Instead he kept his smile firmly in place. It was too early in the morning for this. "What changes do you need?"

"I want both red and green leaf lettuce in the salad, not just green. I want it to look festive."

This was the fifth request he'd had since she'd popped in on him at 7:30 in the kitchen while he briefed Frank on what meals he'd be providing during the rest of the week. She'd followed him in, starting with a request for a revision in plans for the manicures, followed by other changes, and now this lettuce thing.

Instead of massaging the headache he felt brewing, he said, "I thought you had requested a Caesar salad for the meal."

She looked at him with her eyebrows raised nearly to her hairline.

"Of course we can have whatever you'd like," he said, stifling a groan. "Red and green leaf lettuce it is." He made a note on his clipboard, wishing he'd given in to Adele's demands to use an electronic device to download info and keep everyone connected and updated. It would be so much easier than the five things he had crossed out and rewritten this morning. He'd have to add them to his spreadsheet when he returned to his office, and then print out new lists. Poor wasted trees.

"Good." She stalked off through the library room archway but didn't get far before Chelsea intercepted her. The two sisters tangled for a moment, waltzing to get out of each other's way, until Chelsea saw him standing there. Then she turned Belinda around and hustled her back over his way.

This could either go very well or very, very poorly. He braced himself for either, watching the way Chelsea came toward him with her nearly mesmerizing hip swing. He snapped out of it a moment before he'd have embarrassed himself by drooling. Really, he was too old to be affected like this.

He warily watched the approach of the two women, not sure if he was going to get blasted for not giving Chelsea's sister everything she wanted or if he would be in the midst of a fight between the two. He'd done both before. He enjoyed neither. The look on Chelsea's face and the mulish expression on Belinda's made him realize he probably wasn't going to enjoy it this time, either.

"What did she change?" Chelsea demanded as soon as they were within touching distance.

"Hello to you, too, and good morning."

"I don't have time for that," she said, waving his sarcasm away with the flick of her wrist. "Tell me what she changed so I can filter it through her fiancé's reasoning."

Belinda harrumphed, crossing her arms over her chest, obviously not happy. But she hadn't said anything yet.

"Did you want to know what she changed right now or all the things she's asked to change since 7:30?" he asked innocently. He did not want to piss off his client, but he didn't want to take Chelsea by surprise, either.

Chelsea gave him the same raised eyebrows Belinda had, but for some reason they looked softer on Chelsea. Then again, everything looked good on Chelsea.

"All of them." She, too, crossed her arms. The two sisters looked like lush, ultra-feminine bookends except for their hair. Chelsea's was soft and short instead of trailing down her back. She cleared her throat, getting him back on task.

Reading from his clipboard, he listed the things Belinda had changed this morning. "She wants fresh flowers in her room both the night before the wedding, when she moves in, and the morning after the wedding."

Chelsea raised one eyebrow higher than the other, but he continued.

"Instead of going to get manicures on the previously scheduled day, she would like to go the morning of the wedding, to preserve the beauty of the work."

That got a muffled snort.

"Every person is to receive a packet of bird seed, and she would like those finished today."

Now Chelsea's foot started tapping, but she uncrossed her arms and held onto Belinda's arm as if to keep her from escaping.

"She would like for me to arrange to have cans tied to the back of Marcus's car, and a big sign that reads 'Just Married' attached above them."

"Oy!"

"And she wants festive red and green leaf lettuce instead of the Caesar. We have yet to discuss dressings, though, so I can't update you on that." He fought to keep his laughter in check while Chelsea looked at Belinda and then looked back at him with an expression that fully conveyed her exasperation.

"Unmake all those notes you already made, and let's start over again."

Belinda's eyes widened. "Chelsea, you can't do

this!"

"Oh, yes, I can. Especially since you specifically asked me to stop you if you went off the deep end with ridiculous requests." She turned back to Jack and he felt the full power of her gaze. "Let's start with number one. You do not want fresh flowers brought to your room on the morning after the wedding, because hopefully you will be asleep with your new husband after a night of unimagined passion." She gave Jack a cheeky smile that he shared as he went down the rest of the list with her.

****

Chelsea tried hard to keep her cool while dealing with all the things her sister was attempting to change at the last minute. At least she had warned Jack ahead of time that Belinda would be difficult. She should have specifically told him that all changes needed to be filtered through herself, though. After the bridal party finished the delicious quiche Frank had made, she spent over an hour finalizing all the details with them, often over Belinda's strident demands for everything to be different.

And now Chelsea took a moment to lean her hip against the banister after sending Belinda on her way. Chelsea had a headache just thinking about the handful of days left until Saturday. Thankfully it was almost over.

This attraction she felt for Jack every time she was within breathing distance didn't help. She could smell the woodsy scent and something uniquely him, feel it caressing her skin along with his gaze now that they were alone again.

"I'm really sorry about that," she said, hoping to

break the tension sitting thick in the air whenever she let him get near her.

"Believe me, it's not the worst thing that's ever happened here." He laughed, a rumble that vibrated along her skin. He should not affect her like this, and yet she felt helpless against the onslaught.

"Well, I had hoped to avoid it, though I was pretty sure it was going to happen anyway. I think I have her under control now, after everyone ganged up on her at breakfast."

"Believe me, it's not a big deal. But I wish you had told me she needed to go through you first. It would have left me free the other four times she tried to change everything today. She was after me all morning."

Groaning, she put her hand to her forehead, then felt the slight roughness of his hand as it took hers and held it between both of his own. She should pull back out of his personal space, but she couldn't seem to make herself take the step her head knew was best for her.

"It's really nothing. I expected something like this, so I wasn't surprised."

She laughed. "I sure hope you put combat pay into your prices, then, because I have a feeling you have not seen the last of her, no matter what I think I accomplished at breakfast." Now she did finally take her hands from his, tucking them around her waist as she crossed her arms. "Let me know if she tries to change anything again, and we'll get it sorted out." She shook her head ruefully. "I knew this was not going to be the vacation she promised me it would be."

He didn't try to hold her hands again, but he did

rest a gentle palm on her shoulder. "If you'd like, we can go down and have a glass of wine."

Which made her laugh again. She hadn't laughed this much in years. "Except that it's only about 9:30 in the morning. And before you say it, yes, I know it's five o'clock somewhere, but that's not here."

His smile did things to her equilibrium, and she teetered for just a moment, even in her sturdy sneakers. Righting herself was instantaneous, but she still felt a little like she was rocking on the deck of a ship.

Ruthlessly she steadied herself with thoughts of her child and the life she was making for both of them. It enabled her to smile at him and not lean into him the way a part of her wanted to.

"Well, if you're going to pass on the wine, then at least let me say the invitation is open-ended. Perhaps you'll take me up on it another time."

She was the one to reach out this time, laying a hand on his strong forearm. "Jack, I appreciate your concern, but I'm a big girl now. I signed up for this knowing full well what I was getting myself into."

He looked down at her hand, then covered it with one of his own. "You might be older, but that doesn't mean you don't need a shoulder every once in a while. If nothing else, I'd like to be friends again."

Ignoring the "if nothing else," she smiled up at him, feeling a little jittery inside. If it had been another time and another place, another life, she might have jumped at the chance. But she had this life and this time and wouldn't miss out on Mazzy for anything in the world.

"Thank you, Jack, but I've got it." And she walked away. It was a lot harder than it should have been.

****

Two hours later, Jack found himself down in his speakeasy with Chelsea. Mazzy was in the library playing with her grandmother after being bribed with another round of board games against him in the afternoon.

He had been dragooned into hanging large plastic tarps on the wall and covering all the furniture with washable linens. Yet he had no idea why he was doing it other than at Chelsea's request. The place looked like he was closing up a summer home for the winter.

Until right now, he hadn't realized how big this part of the house truly was. But while he was blindly trying to make sure every available surface had some sort of covering on it, it struck him as huge. The bar was cleaned off and covered. Pictures that had hung on the walls for all the years he'd been here were either taken down or covered. The enormous mirror on the far wall had been completely hidden with two shower curtains. The bottles of alcohol had been taken down from their shelves, boxed, and tucked away in a closet.

"So why are we doing this, again?" he asked, pulling a thumbtack from his handy piece of cardboard and sticking it into the corner of yet another sheet of plastic. This one covered the door to the storage cellar where he kept all the paper supplies he stocked up on throughout the year. There was nothing worse than being out of toilet paper in a storm, especially with a house full of guests. He'd never make that mistake again.

"I already cleared it with Paige on the phone, earlier. She said it was fine and for you not to worry. Besides, I can't tell you or I'd have to kill you." She mumbled the words around a tape dispenser stuck between her teeth, but he was pretty sure that was what she said.

"Somehow I can't believe telling me would be a killing-worthy offense. I do have to ask if you're going to ruin anything." He didn't want to sound like a jerk, but he had to know.

"I hope not, so therefore we are putting up plastic to make sure of it."

"Are you going to be throwing water balloons? Balls of shaving cream? Mud wrestling?"

"Nope, nope, and not even close." She quirked an eyebrow at him. "Where do you come up with such ideas?"

"Well, when you won't tell me, and make it sound like a state secret, I can't help but wonder. And I have a very fertile imagination." Nothing proved that better to him than the fact that he was standing here wondering what she would look like with her voluptuous body in a bikini and slathered with chocolate pudding.

The vision itself was, of course, ridiculous, but he had fun with the thought for a moment before clearing his throat. Many years ago he'd seen her get into a huge mudslinging fight at the lake with a few of her friends at the camp where they were counselors. Obviously, it had done things to him that lasted past his adolescence.

"It might seem stupid to you, but I really have to make sure it's not something that's going to hurt the house. I don't think I have enough dishes in the house for you to wash to work off any damage that would need this much plastic. So if you could just tell me..."

He was wheedling, but she had truly piqued his curiosity.

Her impressive chest rising and falling, she huffed out a breath. "If you absolutely must know, we're going to be doing some original wall art for Belinda's new house. She likes to have very different and unique pieces on her plain white walls. She hasn't mentioned it since she said something in passing almost a year ago when she got engaged, but I wrote it down at the time. I thought this would be the perfect time to work on the project with the women who love her most. Then we'll frame them and sign them. They'll be presents that will last a lifetime. Much longer than a toaster or a set of frying pans." She dusted her hands together. "Sorry it's not kinkier."

He returned the smile that popped out on her face. "Mud is much kinkier."

"Mud is much dirtier. I clearly remember not being able to get that gunk out of my hair for almost a week after camp. You know, that time when Alicia Fristsen started throwing mud at me because she wanted to be your girlfriend." Her hands flew over the plastic, tucking it here and moving it there.

Grabbing a cardboard box from under the table, she began unloading tubes and tubes of paint and tray after tray of brushes. She was obviously serious about what they were doing. Hopefully, she was as organized with the sitting room they still had to decorate for the bridal shower afternoon tea.

"I thought the two of you were friends and just having a play fight," he said.

She chuckled. "Ah, boys, so naïve, so trusting that what they see is what they get."

"Hey, now, I might have to take offense here." With his foot on a short stepping stool at the base of the last wall, he gave her a mock scowl.

A stray cinnamon-colored curl escaped the headband she'd put her new hairdo up in, teasing her temple and him at the same time. "You can take whatever you want, but the plain truth is everyone thought you were after me and she would not believe it wasn't true."

But it had been true. Didn't she remember their kiss on the last night of camp, at the dance for just the counselors? He couldn't have dreamt that up. It had been so much harder that year, once they were back at home. But he had put it aside and been her buddy again because he didn't want to lose her altogether, and he didn't want to cause waves between Paige and Chelsea, or between Paige and himself. It had been one kiss that he had chalked up to an experiment gone wrong.

"Interesting," he said, because he really couldn't think of anything else that wouldn't sound hokey over ten years later.

There was that quirked eyebrow again. He was beginning to liken it to a challenge of some sort.

"What?"

"Interesting?" she asked, her hands on her hips. "Interesting? That's all you can say, when I took a mouthful of lake silt over a relationship that never actually happened?"

"Would you take my sincere apology?"

"I would if it was really sincere." She turned back to put another piece of tape on a large sheet of white paper, then stuck the whole thing up on the wall above one of the booths.

Another sheet was secured to the table top. Now he saw the advisability of the plastic. That table was solid oak, and while it would survive paint, he wouldn't want it ruined.

"It really is sincere. In fact…" Against his better judgment, he took the plunge. "You didn't take that silt for nothing. Alicia wasn't wrong."

While she laughed in the act of turning, the sound abruptly stopped when she faced him. His expression was as sincere and serious as he could make it.

****

Well, that was certainly not what she had expected to come from their trip down memory lane. It had been harmless fun to recall days gone by, days when she didn't have all the baggage she carried now. But his full mouth was no longer smiling and his blue eyes no longer crinkled. He looked entirely too serious.

She did what she could to lighten the moment that should have never happened. Why did she always seem to step right into it?

"Come on! I would have known if you harbored a crush on me. We grew up together. The three of us were inseparable that summer, but it was all buddy-buddy stuff. Not anything to get smacked in the face with dirt over. I was so much younger than you, and Paige would have killed me if we'd dated. You never looked at me that way. I was always just that kid Paige hung out with." She really wished Mazzy would escape from Grammy and come downstairs about now to get her out of this extremely awkward conversation.

"Maybe not for you, but I was definitely into you that summer."

"Cut it out. You were not." Her face felt flushed, so she turned away just in case she was turning red. And why she should be embarrassed now, all these years later, was a mystery to her. A whole lifetime had nearly passed since then. Even if he had wanted her with his seventeen-year-old heart, that had no bearing on today at all.

But if it were true, then she had made a terrible mistake in bringing it up. And their fake engagement could be that much more awkward.

She felt his presence behind her, a solid wall of man, heat emanating from him in a way she shouldn't feel through her T-shirt and jean shorts. She dared not turn around when she heard a soft step bringing him even closer. The hair on the nape of her neck tingled. She was torn between leaning back and running away.

His breath was warm on her cheek a second later, a second where she still couldn't decide what she wanted more, for him to back off or to move in closer.

"Don't you remember that kiss?" he asked in a soft voice, husky and way too appealing. "We were dancing to a really old Madonna song from the eighties, something about being crazy, we were standing arm's length apart because of that stupid personal-space rule, and we were shuffling from side to side when I leaned forward and kissed you."

She stood up straight, twisting around and almost knocking him right in the nose. "Oh, my God! I do remember that. I thought you were leaning in to make fun of the way Missy Cartwright was dancing, so I turned my ear toward where I thought you were going to whisper and instead your lips landed on mine. You jumped back so fast I thought it was an accident." She put her hand over her mouth to muffle her laughter. "That was a kiss?"

He took a step back. "Well, it was supposed to be."

Between his disgruntled words and the way he shoved his hands in his pockets, he looked adorable. The urge to pat him on the arm and assure him "no harm, no foul" was nearly overwhelming, but she was all too aware of the fragile male ego.

"That rewrites history for me then, Jack. Thank you."

His frown turned into a look of bafflement. She did pat him on the arm this time.

"I always thought Jake Betancourt was my first kiss. It was a disastrous episode in tenth grade, with slobbering and sucking noises that made me a little ill. Now I know it was you, and that makes life just a little bit sweeter. Thanks. Then and now."

He looked disgruntled when he said, "You're welcome."

"Oh, Jack, don't look so pouty. As far as kisses went, I'm sure it was wonderful. Or would have been if I had understood what was going on."

He grumbled again, and Chelsea thought for a moment about lifting up on her toes to kiss him on the cheek, but that would be skating too close to the edge of reason. No matter how squishy she was feeling inside to know her first kiss had been something much more romantic than Jake Betancourt and his wandering hands of doom.

Putting her hands back on her hips, she stepped back before she could do anything foolish. "All right, I think we're mostly done here. I have a box of gift bags upstairs I'd like to put together, if you have a flat surface I could use. I know Frank is working in the kitchen and everyone is out and about, but I'd like to try to get them done in secret if possible. Do you have somewhere I could go?"

"Of course. There's a linen room on the second floor. It has a folding counter. No one should bother you, since it's not laundry day." He gestured up the stairs with a sweeping hand.

She felt more on even footing again and graced him with a smile as her world gently rested back where it belonged. Thank God she hadn't done anything stupid like kiss him on the cheek. She hadn't touched him—other than the pat on the arm—much better for her unsteady equilibrium.

And that was the last clear thought she had before Jack said, "Damn it," and pulled her into his strong arms, his lips unerringly landing square on hers.

****

It took a moment for Chelsea to kiss him back, but when she did Jack held on for the ride. Her lips were soft and pliant beneath his. Her hands snaked around to his back, holding him at the waist. A small shudder ran through her body and his own responded in kind. Somehow he had known Chelsea Moore would be a good kisser, despite that dismal try in the past. He was very gratified to find out he was more than right. Soft in all the places she should be, she curved into him and they fit like two parts of a whole. However, he didn't get to enjoy the pleasure for long. She pulled back with a gasp just as they were getting to the good part.

Her touch and taste had made him oblivious to his surroundings to the point he'd missed the little girl who came trundling down the stairs while he was lost in Chelsea. But he couldn't miss the way Chelsea separated herself from him, stepping back with her left hand tucked around her ribcage. And he couldn't miss the way her other hand fell on her daughter's shoulder as the little girl took a step toward him.

"My turn for kisses!" she yelled, ducking out from under her mother's hand and launching herself at his knees.

She tugged at his pants until he knelt down to her level. All the while he kept an eye on Chelsea. She just shook her head and blew out a breath.

While he didn't know what that meant, he was distracted from it by the small fry standing in front of him with her hands clasped in front of her narrow chest.

"My turn, Big Man. I want my kisses! Maybe you'll turn into my prince."

"I highly doubt that," he heard Chelsea mutter under her breath.

He ignored her. He'd felt something in that kiss before she pulled away. Whether she'd admit it or not was a dilemma for a different day.

Down on one knee, he took Mazzy's hands from her chest and held them loosely in his own, marveling at how truly small they were. With a gentle brush of his lips, he kissed each of her cheeks in turn.

"Mommylove always kisses my nose, too."

So he kissed her nose. Placing his hands on his knees, he moved to stand up, but Mazzy's hands captured his face and gave him a smacking kiss on his cheek.

"Just for you," she said, before she giggled and went back to her mom's side to hide with her hand covering her eyes.

He cleared his throat, then said, "Thank you," and continued straightening up to his full height. Towering over Chelsea and her daughter, he didn't know how to move beyond this moment.

He searched Chelsea's eyes, but she gave nothing away as she told him, "Well, I guess I'd better let you get back to what you were doing."

At this point he couldn't even remember what that was. Until he looked around at all the plastic and recalled the painting party. Which brought his life back into focus.

He had an inn to run and guests to keep happy and satisfied for the upcoming wedding. Flirting was not on the schedule. They also had a fake engagement that he desperately wanted to be real right here and right now. Dangerous territory, Barton.

Grateful for the reminder, he took a mental and physical step back from the two females in front of him. He could not forget his goals or Chelsea's continued reminders that this was all fake and for just a week. No matter how good she had felt in his arms, she had a life elsewhere, concerns that were not his. He had the inn. That was enough for him.

****

With her lips still warm from Jack's kiss, Chelsea fought the urge to touch them just to see if they were really as swollen as they felt. He'd kissed her thoroughly, more thoroughly than she had been kissed in years, and he'd made her insides quiver. And they'd quivered further when he'd taken her daughter's hands as if she were precious, giving in to her demand in a way he hadn't been required to.

But now they stood in a strange triangle she wasn't sure how to break without cracking something inside herself.

Leave it to Mazzy, though.

"Big Man wants to take me upstairs to get my wooby and a snack, don't you, Big Man?"

Chelsea face heated. "Oh, sweetie," she began, but got cut off.

"Absolutely, Miss Mazzy. Our guests have their requests filled here. I bet Frank has something that's just right for you—if it's all right with your mom?" With his inquiring gaze zeroed in on her face, she was helpless to feel anything but confusion.

"You don't have to do that," she said in a low voice.

But instead of answering, he held out a hand for Mazzy. She jumped at him, grasping his hand as if she were sure of him and that he would take care of her. Chelsea wasn't so sure, yet there was a part of her that wished she could be sure, that she could trust.

But she'd tried once before, and it hadn't worked out. In fact, that was an understatement. It hadn't just not worked out, it had been disastrous. Something she was still picking up the pieces from.

"Please, Mommylove!" Mazzy pleaded. "Big Man will take care of me, and Mr. Frank wants to feed me. I just know it!"

Chelsea had to laugh at her audacity. "I'm sure Mr. Frank would love to feed you when you had breakfast only a little while ago. Isn't the kitchen getting ready for lunch, Jack?"

"I know people," he said with a wink. "I'll find something for her if Frank has too much going on."

"And is that part of the price I pay for staying here? To have you wait on my daughter? Or will I owe extra?"

His eyes gleamed for just a second with an emotion

she was unwilling to put a name to.

"Call it a favor for an old friend." He shrugged. "I'll find your mom after we're done. Then I'll be back, once Mazzy is settled, to help you with the rest. Or you can get ready for the afternoon in peace. Your choice."

Her choice. She hadn't had choices in a long time. "I can start getting the room upstairs finished up by myself, if you don't mind. I'll let you know if I need you." This way she'd still have his help if necessary but wouldn't be in the same room with him alone again just yet. She was going to need a little time to get herself back on an even keel. And she could trust Jack with her daughter even if she couldn't trust herself with him. And wasn't that going to make for an awkward engagement? "I'll call my mom right now and have her meet you in the kitchen." She pulled out her cell phone and had her finger hovering over the speed dial.

"Tell her to take her time if she's in the middle of something. We'll be fine, won't we, Mazzy?"

"Yep. Just fine. Bye, Mommy, bye!" And her baby dragged the man up the stairs without a backward glance.

Chelsea dropped her cell phone down to her side and bounced it against her thigh a few times. Waiting to call her mom might be a good idea until she got herself calmed down. She didn't want to sound as breathless as she still felt from that kiss. Jack might not have known how to kiss properly when he was younger, but he certainly knew what he was doing now.

Groaning, Chelsea thumped her head against the wall. What had she gotten herself into? This was a huge mistake. Only three more days.

Reminding herself of that a few more times helped.

But then her mom came down the stairs and her calm washed away as the older woman quirked an eyebrow at her.

"Were you planning on using that phone or is it a prop so you can keep your hands to yourself with Jack when Mazzy's around?"

Oh, Lord. "I was just going to call you."

"I see that." She smiled a Cheshire-cat smile.

"I really was. Jack took Mazzy upstairs to get her a snack, and I wanted to see if you could help with some of the things for the party."

"He's so good with her, honey." Chelsea found herself in a tight embrace. "I'm so happy you found him. And it's not going to hurt Mazzy to see a healthy relationship. I know I don't know all the parts and pieces of your relationship with Paul. But I know enough to know it wasn't a good one. You want Mazzy to have a healthy outlook on love. Now she'll have all of us to see how it can work."

She had to get her mother out of here. It was unbearable to have these conversations. Thankfully it was only a few more days, and she'd have to pick up the acting if she wanted her mom to think it was real for that amount of time. She didn't think she was going to have to fake the heartbreak as she drove away from here.

****

Frank and a bunch of his buddies were in the kitchen when Jack pushed through the swinging door. Jack had a strict no-smoking policy in his inn, and Frank and his poker buddies followed it to the letter. But they still chewed on their unlit cigars while staring hard at their cards. Wednesday midmorning was not their usual poker time, but with all the activities and extra duties, Frank had agreed to move it up. Jack had forgotten it was today, but it shouldn't be a problem.

After Jack cleared his throat, Frank jumped to attention. His green plastic visor circled his balding head and the armbands at his biceps were garters he claimed were from women he knew back in the day. He was quick to drop the cigar.

Just not quick enough.

"Smoking is very, very bad for you, Mr. Frank!" The tiny girl shook her finger at the grizzled man. "What would your mommy say if she knew you were doing bad things?"

Frank had the grace to flush, and his six friends dropped their own cigars within seconds of each other.

"All gone now, Mazzy," Jack said, but had to grin at the way she still stood with her fists on her hips and a scowl on her face.

"That's very bad. I learned it on the cartoon, and Mommy told me. Didn't your mommy learn you that too?"

Laughing, Frank scooped her up off the floor, making her whoop with glee. "Yes, my mommy learned me that, but I guess I forgot. Now what can I do for my helper? You need a snack? Should we give one to Mr. Big Man, too? Has he been a good boy today?"

"He sure has! He gave me three kisses and let me kiss him. I told him he had to because Mommy wasn't the only one who wanted kisses from Big Man. I should get kisses, too, right? Right?"

"Big Man kissed your mommy?"

Jack nearly buried his head in his hands. He should have said something to Mazzy about not repeating that information. Frank knew the engagement wasn't real and so did Adele, but that was it. Then again, how do you tell a precocious four-year-old to not mention something? He had a gut feeling she wouldn't have listened anyway. And she'd want to know why she couldn't say anything. He was not going to be the one to introduce her to lying.

"Yep." She smooshed Frank's grizzled cheeks between her palms, then pulled at a couple of his whiskers. "You're scratchy. Why are you so scratchy? Big Man isn't. Don't you shave? My mom doesn't have to shave her face, but her legs get hairy and she has to shave those. Her armpits, too."

Muffled laughter sounded behind him and Jack tried to suppress his own chuckle. Man, she was something else.

"Let's get Frank to give you a snack, and then you and I can go into the parlor. We can play a game until your grandmother comes to get you."

"But I want to stay with Mr. Frank."

"Now, sugar, Mr. Frank's friends are here today and then he has to make tea for this afternoon. They're playing a grown-up game of their own. You can have your snack, and then maybe you can beat me at Candyland again. I'm not a bad loser, right?"

Anything to get her out of here and himself away from the twinkling in Frank's eyes. Adele would know by this afternoon that he had kissed a guest. He'd have to brace himself for her to light into him the way he had lit into her when she had become involved with a man who stayed here for two months to write a book. He was not going to hear the end of this from either of them. A breather would be nice before it got really bad.

"You're a good loser! I bet I could play Go Fish here, though. Do you want to learn Go Fish? I win that one, too." She smooshed Frank's face again. He had new wrinkles and a lot more patience than Jack had ever thought he possessed.

"Tell you what, kid," Frank said in his gruff voice. "I'll let you teach me Go Fish tomorrow after the breakfast dishes are done. How about that? You go beat Big Man at your game today and we'll play our game tomorrow."

A disgruntled look came over her face, her brow scrunching and her bottom lip sticking out. Frank tugged on that protruding lip. "Should we see if I can wrap that big lip around your head?"

"No! You're silly!" she shrieked, giggling and squirming. "You should let me down now so I can get my snack and beat the Big Man."

He and Frank exchanged a look as she automatically reached for chocolate chip cookies. Frank gently nudged her toward a pumpkin cookie. He'd told Jack earlier he was trying out a new recipe. It was made from all organic ingredients. It had little sugar, was made with applesauce, and would be actually almost good for her. Almost. At least Chelsea would probably approve.

The mere thought of Chelsea made him take the seat Frank had vacated. It brought back the kiss they'd shared in the speakeasy. No way would she be able to mistake that one for an accident. And yet he didn't know how he felt about it, or the way he'd impulsively taken the kiss as far as he could, or how much he'd enjoyed it.

He thought she enjoyed it, too, but something

inside told him he was probably not going to get another one anytime soon. And he shouldn't want one, he told himself as he watched Mazzy suck down her pumpkin cookie. He didn't need the complications or the added weight of anyone else when he'd just started getting the inn in order, and his life with it. He had a good setup here. One he wasn't willing to mess up for a kiss or two. Especially because Chelsea was a package deal. This little girl was a handful and wonderful, but he didn't think he was ready to take on a readymade family even if Chelsea was willing. Which apparently she was not.

Mazzy brought him back from his musings by climbing into his lap. He didn't know where to hold her, where to put his hands, so he did what felt right and put one on her shoulder, using the other to hold her legs on his lap. She snuggled her head into his chest and sighed.

"I like you, Big Man. You're not squishy like Mommy, but you're comfy."

"Thanks," he said, baffled. He had to move on to the game portion of this afternoon before he got sucked into this little girl's charm.

He lifted her and set her on her feet, and she thanked Frank with her cheeky smile, then gave him one more warning about smoking. Without another word, she skipped out of the kitchen.

She was going to be a killer when she grew up. Just like her mom was now and had been when they were younger. He'd missed the in-between years because she hadn't come home, but he was thankful he had gotten a chance to see Chelsea again finally. And that kiss was worth a little angst because he'd finally gotten her out of his system. The one thing he'd wished he'd done all those years ago was finally a done deal.

Now if only he could convince himself he didn't want just one more taste.

Chapter Seven

Bustling around the sitting room where the second part of the bridal shower would be held, Chelsea put last-minute touches on the mantel of the fireplace and the small round table Paige had asked Jack for on one of her many lists. Flower petals of dark purple and rich red rested on the sand-colored linens Jack had also had on hand. She'd brought the chocolate kisses, but Jack had supplied the cut crystal bowls and the beautiful jewel-toned cloth napkins. Jack had also made sure the petals smelled faintly so as not to overpower but enhance.

Jack, Jack, Jack. Chelsea's hand drifted up to her mouth for about the thirtieth time before she planted it on her hip. She would not touch her lips again. In fact, she would not think about that kiss at all, since it would never happen again, shouldn't have happened in the first place. Fake engagement or not, kissing had not been part of the bargain.

"You look lost in thought," Chelsea's mother said from the doorway to the sitting room.

Chelsea was quick to pull her face into an innocent expression. She would not share anything with her mom about Jack. What could she say? Supposedly they had already been kissing before now, and she had gotten the tingles plenty of times. Enough, anyway, to want to marry him. Sharing that the first—or technically second—time he'd kissed her in their whole lives had rocked her foundation would not go over well.

"Just making sure I have everything I need," Chelsea answered, running her hand over the violet ribbons she'd twined through the fresh oak branches already decorating the fireplace. Jack had good taste, or a great interior designer.

And there she went about Jack again.

"And do you?" her mom asked, bringing her back to the conversation.

"Do I what?" But she registered the question a half second later. "Oh, yes, I have everything we need for this afternoon. Is Snazzy Mazzy ready to come into the basement and make her very own painting?"

"Yes, I had to let her walk Big Man back to the kitchen after she trounced him several more times at the board games. Then she wanted me to see your room and let her escort Belinda down, since it was a very important job." Her mother gave a soft laugh. "You are going to have your hands full when she gets older. Happy Mother's Day to me."

"You just love saying that."

Leigh's Happy Mother's Day came more often than once a year. It came every time she chortled with glee over something that, to her, was payback for Chelsea's younger years.

"And I'll probably say it for all the years my Mazzy is growing up, too, but you know I love you, honey, and she's a really good child. Just precocious."

"That's one way of putting it. But I'd do anything for her." Chelsea watched Mazzy lead Belinda down the stairs, keeping a tight grip on her hand and telling her to watch her step. A buzz of excited voices in the foyer filtered up and over her.

She'd separated herself from her family while trying to work things out with Mazzy's father, thinking she couldn't accomplish her goal with her family's interference. It was a terrible decision, one of many, and one she was still trying to make up for with her family. After Paul left, money was too tight even with child support, keeping her job too important, to get away even for a weekend. They had come down to her a few times, but it wasn't the same.

And this was the perfect chance to make amends Despite how everyone assured her they'd understood her decision to concentrate on just Paul and Mazzy, she'd still felt the distance. Helping with the wedding was a huge step toward bridging the gap, and one she felt was going well. She wasn't going to accomplish more than that by mooning over Jack or even thinking about him.

With her resolve solidified in her mind, she tied a blindfold around Belinda's eyes when she reached the bottom of the stairs, then led everyone down one more set of steps with Belinda's hand in hers.

This time was for her sister, not for an affair that would never go anywhere.

Everything went off wonderfully, for the most part. What should have been fun bonding had turned into some kind of raging hormone fest as Belinda had gone teary, then rambunctious, sullen, then ecstatic and back to teary. Chelsea got that she was probably nervous about getting married, but Belinda had been with Marcus for nine years and they were happy. What was there to be nervous about? They had been dating since seventh grade, for heaven's sake!

Chelsea only hoped this wasn't a precursor to the rest of the next three and a half days.

****

The next day, with the house silent and all the ladies out doing manicures and pedicures, Jack called a staff meeting to be held in the kitchen right before lunch. He needed to touch base with everyone, see how things were running, ask if any of them had been accosted by Belinda, and find out if they had everything they needed.

He brought a list of topics along with him and expected to be interrupted a hundred times before he was done with the hour-long get-together.

But he hadn't counted on being taken to task almost immediately upon entering the kitchen. He had successfully avoided Adele and Frank except for small exchanges in passing. Stupidly, he had thought they'd have forgotten about his indiscretion. Apparently not.

"So, I hear you're kissing a guest now." Adele sat at the small table where Frank and his cronies had been playing poker. Her posture was relaxed; however, her mouth smiled but not her eyes.

Jack knew better than to look to Frank for any help. He was the likeliest person to have spilled the news in the first place.

"It was a mistake and one I won't repeat, not that it's any of your business."

Frank snorted from his place at the counter where he was building Reuben sandwiches.

Jack braced himself against the back of a chair and prepared to pull rank. But Adele beat him to anything he would have said.

"I think she's really sweet and nice. You should go

for her."

"What?" he said, taken aback. After all, he was the one who had dressed her down for getting involved with that writer.

Now the smile reached her eyes. "You heard me. Did you think I was going to tear your head off? She's a very nice woman. She'd make a great innkeeper and a great woman for you. Just as long as I'm not going to lose my job."

"I…we…but…" he sputtered, before he took a deep breath and ordered his thoughts. "It's not like that. I knew her long ago and was proving a point about something from the past."

"With your lips? That's an interesting way to go about proving a point. I'll have to watch out for a disagreement with you. Frank, you should do the same," she said over her shaking shoulder. Her snicker was anything but quiet.

Frank's snicker wasn't, either. "I'll be sure to agree with him from now on. I don't want any points made to me that way. Not that you aren't quite the guy, boss, but you understand I have some limits."

Jack rolled his eyes and clamped a hand to his forehead. This was going to be a nightmare. Unless he made his point now without using a kiss.

Running his hand down his face, he then looked at them. "Look, it was something from the past. If I have to tell you, then I want you both not to mention a word of it in front of Chelsea or her family."

Two eager sets of eyes found his, and the snickering stopped immediately.

"Back when I was a counselor at a summer camp, I tried to kiss her, and she thought it was an accident. I was showing her what I had intended ten years ago."

This time it wasn't snickering, it was all-out laughing. They had a congenial working relationship, almost like a family, since they were all together so often. He should have known better than to put himself in this position. But one look at Chelsea's laughing eyes yesterday seemed to have leaked his brain right out of his ears.

"You can laugh all you want, but do it on your own time. We have situations to take care of and people to care for." It should have come out as a command, but the more he thought about the situation, the more it made him laugh at himself. He shook his head as a chuckle came out. It lasted a while and lightened his heart.

"All right, down to business. Apparently we have to be on our toes with Belinda. I'm going to need you guys on your game."

Groans were followed by avid gazes.

"It's going to be a challenge, but one I think we're all up to. Chelsea and Belinda put a safeguard into effect before coming here. Belinda has to clear any changes with Chelsea before making them. She's on a full-out assault, but Chelsea put Belinda back in her place."

"Bride's already been in here, too," Frank said while he brought the sandwiches to the table.

Jack got his first bite in and down before responding. "What did she want, and did you promise it to her?" He drew his clipboard over to mark things down.

"Eh, she wanted to change the prime rib to salmon. I ain't gonna do that, no matter what, so I put her off.

She's a tough bird, though. Or at least she was until Chelsea came in and ushered her out without a single word. She's even tougher, and that little girl of hers is following close on her heels. I still can't believe she took me to task for smoking even when I wasn't." He chuckled and shook his head.

Adele also shook her head, her bright red hair sifting out around her rounded shoulders. He'd thought at some point he should have just gone for her. She would have been a perfect person to share the inn with. But there was nothing there between them, unlike him and Chelsea. He shook that thought right out of his head.

"This whole family is something else," Adele said. "I like them."

So did he, but that had no bearing on the situation, he reminded himself. "I like them all, too, but we have to keep an eye out for Belinda. We only have a few days left until the wedding, but they are going to be trying if we're fending her off at the same time we're meeting our scheduled obligations. I'll talk to Chelsea and see what can be done." He made a note on his clipboard.

"Just make sure to have a point to get across again, Boss," Frank said with a wink.

Jack sighed and settled in for the rest of the meeting. Sometimes family was overrated.

****

A little over sixty hours until the wedding. Chelsea's mind whirled with all the things that still needed to be done. With her muscles loose and limber from her massage this morning, Chelsea looked into Mazzy's bedroom and smiled at the little girl's sleeping

145

form. She had been so excited to do big-girl things that she'd worn herself out.

Which was fine with Chelsea. Lists yards long waited for her in the drawing room downstairs. How was she going to get all this done? There was a whole sheet of paper with scribbles in the margin that needed her attention, and so much to prepare for the wedding. With that thought, she pocketed the companion to Mazzy's monitor and went down the stairs.

After booting up the laptop, she applied herself to whittling down the list to what was manageable. It wasn't hard, just tedious—so much like her job back home that she did it without really thinking. Being a corporate secretary was nothing to sniff at, but it certainly had not been her lifelong dream when she'd graduated high school and gone to college.

But she had other dreams now. Watching Mazzy grow up. Providing a good life for her daughter. Making up for being only one parent in what should have been a two-parent home. If there wasn't room in those dreams for a man, then that was okay with her. She had plenty to offer Mazzy and had been doing a fine job with her. A kiss from an old friend couldn't change the entire way she had structured her life.

It was changing too much already, in that she was only making short calls to Paige to keep her up to date with the wedding week progress and not spending too much time with her friend, in case she accidently said the wrong thing.

The sound of Mazzy waking up was most welcome. Mazzy was standing on the bed when Chelsea entered their suite, and Chelsea couldn't help but smile even as she gently reprimanded her.

"Come on, Mazzy, what did Mommy say about jumping on the bed?"

"But it's so much fun!' she said, drawing out the last word as she did a particularly big bounce and coughed.

"I asked you to be on your best behavior, though. If you can't do that, then we aren't going to be able to do all the fun things I have planned. And we have to cover our mouths when we cough."

Mazzy's bottom was planted on the bed and her hand covered her mouth before Chelsea finished her sentence. "Sorry! I want to do fun things!" she said, muffled.

"Let's get to it, then. I thought we'd go over to Grammy's and run around for a while."

"Yay!" And Mazzy was off, washing her hands and trying to comb her bed head. Chelsea helped when she got caught in a tangle the knot fairy had kissed into it. She loved the softness of Mazzy's hair and she loved spending time with her daughter. One of the things she had sacrificed by taking on these extra jobs was the ability to just hang with Mazzy for a week. But the little girl was having so much fun with everyone else, Chelsea relaxed her biting guilty conscience. She was spending as much time as possible with her.

Once Mazzy was ready, they bundled into Chelsea's car. Although she hadn't called to announce their visit, she knew her mom was going to be home all day doing some of her own tasks as mother of the bride.

"Come on in, Chelsea," Leigh called out through the screen door on the porch.

"How do you always know?" Chelsea finished her journey up the sidewalk with Mazzy's hand in hers. Her mother was waiting in the four-seasons room Chelsea's parents had built last year, a glass of tea in her hand and a smile on her face.

After exchanging a hug with her mom, she followed Leigh into the light airy house of her childhood.

She marveled at how clean and orderly her mother's house was compared to her own. Then again, her mother's spaces were always clean and orderly whereas Chelsea, while growing up, had had a hard time finding her way out of her bedroom without tripping.

"I have those eyes in the back of my head, dear. Surely you remember me talking about them years ago. Every mother gets them." Leigh turned and smiled, looking much closer to forty than her fifty-five years.

"How did I get passed over, then? I don't feel like I have eyes back there." Taking a seat on her mother's floral couch, Chelsea tried not to mess up the precise lines of the afghan behind her. Each side hit the arms in the exact same place and the design of miniature sprigs of violets was perfectly aligned in the center of the back. Another skill Chelsea did not possess.

"You have them, honey, they just take a bit to focus. How many times have you nabbed Mazzy out of trouble at the last second?" She folded the blanket she'd probably been using to rest in the wing-backed chair next to the fireplace and put it back on the blanket rack. Chelsea would have left hers thrown over the back of the chair.

"That's not the same thing as being able to tell which person is at the door before they announce themselves."

Leigh chuckled. "That's something totally different and has more to do with the fact that you have a different step pattern than anyone else here. I always know when you're walking somewhere near me. Which is why you had such a hard time sneaking out of this house when you were younger."

Chelsea groaned thinking about the two times she had tried it. Both times she'd been caught. But then she laughed. At least she would only have one child to know footsteps for, and they were the only two people in the house, always would be. If she felt a moment of wistfulness at that thought, now was not the time to think about it.

"Okay, I'll take your word for it, though I always thought it was unfair Belinda never got caught."

"Oh, she got caught plenty, which was why she got moved into a different room and had everything taken from her. But you were in college at that point, so you wouldn't have known. However, you didn't come here to rehash the long ago past." Another smile, this one gentle at the edges. "Is it my turn to watch my girl again?" she asked eagerly.

Chelsea shut down the immediate flood of guilt. Her mother loved being with Mazzy and had eagerly jumped at the chance to watch her this week while Chelsea helped Belinda. In fact, she had insisted on it before Chelsea had a chance to ask. But Chelsea had been forced to draw the line at having her mother keep Mazzy in their extra bedroom so that Leigh could watch her twenty-four hours a day.

"You'd probably better give me the monitor and get going. I hear your sister tromping up the stairs. You know she's going to have you in a whirlwind the second she steps in here."

Chelsea shook her head, bracing herself for whatever trouble Belinda was bringing with her.

"I want to go hiking tomorrow," her sister said without preamble or even a hello.

"What?" Chelsea and her mother said at the exact same time.

"Hiking," Chelsea's sister said, jerking her arms into a tight crossing against her chest. "I want to go."

Their mother sputtered in protest, making a ton of valid arguments that fell on absolutely deaf ears. Those ears had been locked down to reason and accompanied eyes that dared Chelsea to say no.

Chelsea stared her down like she would her daughter when she didn't want to take a bath. "We are not going hiking tomorrow. What if you break your leg or your head? What would I tell Marcus if you can't come down the aisle on your own power because you're in a coma?"

Belinda scoffed. "I have never hurt myself hiking. I'm certainly not going to start now. You just don't want to have any fun."

Apparently this would be just like getting Mazzy to do something she didn't want to do, scowling pout and all. Chelsea sighed as a tiny cough came from the next room.

"Look, I don't have time for this today, Belinda. Perhaps we can figure something else out." The mutinous expression on her sister's face didn't change. "Your wedding is on Saturday and tomorrow is Friday. You can't go hiking the day before the wedding."

"I can if I want to."

"You know what, do whatever you want, Belinda. I

signed on to make sure you wouldn't change the menu or the entire color scheme for the wedding in a fit of nervousness before the big day, but I did not sign on for this. Hopefully you won't fall."

And she breezed past her stunned sister, walking briskly to her child. When she arrived in the family room, she hustled toward the couch. Settling lightly next to Mazzy, she laid a hand on her forehead and breathed a sigh of relief when she felt no heat. That was the last thing—besides her sister hiking—she needed. No child was pleasant when they were sick. The little girl coughed again, but it didn't sound too bad. Maybe she was simply over-exhausted from all they had been doing. Most likely that was it.

She called Adele to let her know she might be a few more minutes than she had planned. After kissing Mazzy one more time, she stepped out of the room to talk with her mom.

"I don't think she has a cold, but I'm not sure I should leave now. What if she gets sick?"

"Honey, I have taken care of more colds and coughs than you can imagine. I was a daycare worker for years when you and your sister were little. I can handle this."

"I know, I know, but I don't feel right leaving if she's not feeling well."

"Tell you what. How about if I call you if she starts running a fever? In the meantime, we'll hang out here and see how things go. You have a ton of things to do, Chelsea." Her mom rubbed her arm and gave her a smile. "Go take care of them and let me spend some spoiling time with my granddaughter. I've been looking forward to having her all to myself for a while now."

And there went Chelsea's guilt, again. She'd been working for a promotion over the last six months, and in process had robbed Mazzy of memories in this special house.

"I see that frown, missy, and I want it gone right now." Her mom smoothed her index finger over the crease between Chelsea's eyebrows. "We are always happy to come down to your neck of the woods to visit. Your dad and I like to get out of town every once in a while. But it's going to be so nice to have you here permanently soon. Your dad and I cannot wait!"

"It's nice to be back," Chelsea said. There was no changing the past, so she'd make the future better. Although, how much better was she really going to make it when her mother found out there was no engagement and she and Mazzy were not going to be living here? The lie just got deeper. She'd make it up to her mother somehow, once things settled down with her new promotion back in Bettleton. "I'd like to have come up more often. But what's done is done." She laughed. "First I have to get through this wedding without letting Belinda kill herself."

"I heard that!" Belinda yelled from the other room.

"I meant you to," Chelsea answered.

She hugged her mom again before stopping to glare at Belinda one more time. "Hike if you want, but your dress is going to look funny with a cast under it."

Belinda stuck her tongue out and Chelsea did the same.

Trooping down the stairs to her car, she mentally reviewed everything to be accomplished before the day was out. Belinda was lucky she didn't boot her in the butt, or decide not to help if she was going to be so difficult.

She couldn't stay mad at her sister for long, though. It was fading already as she drove the mile back to the inn.

Belinda had always been headstrong and hated to fail at anything. She did things she knew she could do instead of trying anything new. And marriage probably terrified her no matter how much she loved Marcus.

Entering the inn, Chelsea almost passed right by Jack in her musings until he reached out and snagged her wrist in one of his big hands. She stared down at his warm flesh on hers for a brief second, then shot her gaze back up to his.

The smile on his face was an easy one. He'd been crouched down at the entrance to the coat closet, a close mirror to the linen room on the second floor that she'd used the other night to make the bachelorette party gifts. Thoughts of the party brought a slight blush to her neck and heat to her stomach. She really hoped Jack had not overheard some of the suggestions her cousins and her sister had for what she should do with him.

"Need anything?" he asked, rising but still using his long fingers to lightly encircle her wrist.

"Um, I was looking for Adele to see if she had gotten my voicemail about being late. I need to dive into these lists and told my mother I'd be back later with some cough syrup for Mazzy."

"I believe Adele's upstairs. She should be down in a minute."

But as the words left his mouth, Adele came hacking and wheezing from the back staircase. She looked miserable, with circles under her eyes and her hair thrust untidily into a ponytail.

"Uh-oh," Chelsea breathed, retrieving her hand from Jack's.

"Yeah, you're not kidding," he said to her before turning back to Adele. "Go back upstairs, Adele. I'm giving you the day off, and probably tomorrow, too. You should not be walking around. I'll go get you something from the pharmacy, and I can get your stuff, too, Claudia."

"But we can't let this wedding be ruined." Adele's eyes watered, breaking Chelsea's heart.

"We'll be fine." Jack rose to his full height, gently turning Adele back around by the shoulders. "Just focus on recuperating, lady."

She gave him a watery smile, then turned and trudged back up the stairs.

Chelsea heard Jack mutter a particularly harsh expletive under his breath as if he'd forgotten she was there. From what she'd seen of Adele, she didn't seem to be the type to give in easily, so she must have really been sick.

A second later, Jack composed himself and turned to Chelsea. "Apparently, I'm going to the pharmacy, so if you want to just make me a list of the things you want, I'll get them while I'm out." After running a rough hand over the top of his head and down his neck, he blew out a breath and shoved his hands into his pockets.

Obviously she couldn't know what exactly was going through his mind right at this moment, but it had to go something along the lines of "What in the hell am I going to do now?"

And she felt for him. As she would feel for anyone who was in this kind of predicament. As she'd felt for some of the other secretaries in her office when they were overwhelmed and understaffed in an emergency situation. Now she did the same thing she would have done for any of them.

"Tell me what Adele was doing and I'll fill in for her while she's recuperating."

He opened his mouth, and she could almost see the protest hanging on his tongue.

"Don't say it. I'm going to help whether you want me to or not. This wedding is very important to my sister, and I won't have it ruined because you're too stubborn to accept help."

His mouth snapped shut at that. He gave her a speculative look. Standing ramrod straight under his narrowed gaze, she waited for him to realize she was right. If he was anything like a lot of other males in and out of her life, she could potentially still be standing here next Monday.

"Fine," he said grudgingly. "But you aren't doing a lot. You're still going to have some fun even if I have to dragoon Frank into coming out of the kitchen to act as hostess."

She couldn't help a small smile at the picture he painted. It wouldn't come to that. This could be a different kind of fun if she looked at it correctly. She had organizational skills out the wazoo and a keen eye for exactly what needed to be done, multitasking as well as delegating. Not that she'd have many people to delegate to, but she had enough. And her mom could take care of Mazzy while Chelsea had more of a hand in creating the perfect wedding for her sister. Not a bad deal all the way around. As an added bonus for those watching closely, it could appear she was getting the lay of the land for when she moved here. The thought sent a flutter through her stomach that she resolutely ignored.

"I want a clipboard," she said, holding out her hand.

He removed his from the top closet shelf, passing it to her outstretched hand along with the walkie-talkie on his waistband. "I'll find you one. In the meantime, here's mine. These are the things I wanted Adele to do."

The small plastic walkie-talkie was still warm from being close to his body. She concentrated on the clipboard instead. Letting her eyes scan over the paper, Chelsea prayed she had not bitten off more than she could chew. The list was extensive, but she was also capable. She looked up at him, caught his eye, and nodded. "Will do, Boss Man."

Then she left before he could see how uncertain she felt in her new self-proclaimed role. Holy heck, she hoped she didn't fall apart before it was all done.

Chapter Eight

The drive to the pharmacy gave Jack time to settle. Of course Adele had been sick before, and so had he. They weren't immune to colds, but they'd never had a shindig this big. So of course it had to happen now.

He was trying to keep his cool, but the details kept piling up in his head. He prayed Chelsea would be able to help him. At first he had given her the clipboard to pacify her, but once he'd gone over things in his head, he knew he'd need help. He was tempted to pull out his cell phone and call someone—anyone. But he didn't want to bother his parents during their vacation and he couldn't think of anyone else he trusted as much. At least Chelsea had a stake in the outcome. That should buoy her along to do an excellent job. He'd have to give serious thought to waiving her bill if this all came together.

He parked his car in front of the small, privately owned pharmacy that had been doing business since the 1800s. They'd kept the original décor and many of the original prescriptions ranged in vintage apothecary jars on high shelves above the work area. The bell rang over his head as he opened the front door, announcing his arrival to the three people in the store.

He waved casually to the pharmacist in his white coat, nodded politely to the blue-haired lady who came to a book club at the inn the first Tuesday of every month, and tried to duck into the shadows to avoid the third person.

He was successful with the last for all of about two minutes, just long enough to hope he'd gotten the right cough suppressant for a four-year-old. Minnie Daley trooped down the cold remedy aisle with purpose in her stride and fire in her eyes.

"I hear Adele's sick." Her legs were a mile long and her figure was something to lust over. But her personality made those attributes about as tempting as a moldy cookie.

Pretending he hadn't heard wasn't an option. He turned from perusing the cold medicines to face her, not startled to see her in a skirt that ended about eight inches above her knees.

News traveled fast in this small town. "Nice to see you, too."

"Of course, it's nice to see you, Jack," she purred in what she probably thought was a sultry voice. Instead it made him feel like he was strapped into a chair with some sadistic bastard dragging nails down a chalkboard. He stepped out of the way unobtrusively as she lifted one paw—um, hand—toward him.

"I'm getting married," he blurted before his brain caught up with his tongue.

"Really?" she purred again. "I don't see a ring on my finger, and I know it's not to anyone else." She lifted her own bare left hand and wagged it at him.

Her perfectly manicured claws landed on the shelf next to his arm, almost trapping him. But he had done this dance a million times. He would have thought his announcement would have put her off, but apparently nothing was off limits to Minnie. She'd chased before and she chased now. Ever since his parents had left him with the inn Minnie desperately wanted to run, she'd been relentless.

"I was just thinking you might need some help over there at that big ol' house with all those out-of-towners. We could do it right, Jack." She gave him a slow wink showing the overabundance of teal on her eyelid. He got her double entendre but pretended he hadn't.

At that moment he thought of Chelsea and how natural she was, how much more he appreciated her subtle beauty and her unadorned face. He had bigger problems right now. He had to put Minnie off or the woman would show up at the inn with her luggage and her own ideas.

"Actually I have my fiancée Chelsea up at the inn, Minnie. I'm sure you remember Chelsea from high school. I appreciate your offer, but it's unnecessary. She's getting her feet wet regarding what it takes to keep an event rolling, and she's doing a fine job." He almost choked on the last word. He manned up before he got himself into trouble. "Besides I'm sure Adele will be back to her normal self in no time and running things with her usual efficiency shortly after that."

Minnie got a look on her face that very clearly told Jack she was about to make a scene and steamroll over him. But Carl Wendell saved him and earned himself a free weekend at the inn when all this craziness was over. Jack made a mental note to find out when the man's anniversary was and let him and his wife celebrate at the inn.

"I have that medicine ready for ya, Minnie," Carl said, risking his life and limbs to put a hand under her elbow, moving her back to the counter. Behind his back, he waved Jack out the door.

Jack knew a save when he saw one. He booked it out of the store. Carl would simply put his things on his tab. He wasn't a coward, but there were some things you did not mess with in this life. Minnie could be relentless.

And he'd just told her he was getting married to Chelsea even though Chelsea had wanted to keep the people who knew to a minimum. This was not going to be pretty.

Jumping back into his car, he cranked the engine, then headed back the way he had come. He would not admit even to himself that the prospect of seeing Chelsea was one of the reasons his foot was a little heavier on the gas pedal than normal.

****

Taking a moment to use a pencil from the front desk to wind her hair up into a small bun, Chelsea got to work on the list Jack had left her. Looking at the jobs, she prioritized them, and was interrupted when her cell phone went off in her pocket.

She hadn't had the guts to let her mom know what she was doing just yet, because she knew what Leigh would say. She would crow with delight that Chelsea was stepping in early to make herself at home. She just didn't know how much farther she could carry this lie that had blossomed into a garden of snarly weeds.

Also, it was going to be tricky to handle both Mazzy and her own duties for the wedding along with this new set of requirements. Not to mention that she was still hiding the fake engagement from Paige, and Belinda was going to blow a gasket if she thought Chelsea was doing anything more than making the perfect wedding.

Sighing over her reluctance to talk to her mom was not going to help her. So she took a seat on the stairs to wait for voicemail to kick in and allowed herself a moment to work up the nerve to hit her mom with a request for even more of her time.

Jack came in the front door at that moment, giving her a reason to put off the call for another moment or two.

"Hey," he said. His hands were full of plastic bags. Nudging the front door closed with his hip, he turned to her. "Here's the shampoo. I also picked up a few things for Mazzy to keep her busy. I figured it was the least I could do when you're helping me. I want you to know she can run around here all she wants. I really appreciate everything."

"You didn't have to do that." She opened one of the two bags he'd handed her and found crayons, coloring books, a stuffed rabbit, and a jump rope. Wow.

"I almost bought her a bike with training wheels at a garage sale on my way back, but I didn't know how far along she was on that."

Chelsea literally felt her heart melt and did everything she could to firm it back up. Paul had never bought Mazzy anything after she'd been born. Mazzy didn't even have a bike because Chelsea hadn't had time or the room to teach her how to ride. Tears burned the back of her eyes, but she willed them away.

"This is plenty, Jack, more than enough, actually. You didn't even have to do this much. A bike might have been overkill." Especially because it would have definitely made her cry. "I'll run these things over to my mom's now, if you don't need me at the moment.

I'm going to ask her to keep Mazzy for the duration. She'll be thrilled." And Chelsea would try not to be lonely.

She touched Jack's sleeve on her way out the door, not trusting herself to hug him the way she wanted to.

"One last thing." His lengthy pause had her turning toward him. "I told a few people in town we are getting married."

Her heart stopped. That snarly little bed of weeds had just turned into a choking jungle. "You what?"

Clamping his hand over his eyes, he sighed. "Minnie tried to corner me in the pharmacy. She wanted to come help me run the inn since Adele was sick. She's had her eyes on this place from the time my parents turned it over to me, and she wants her hooks in me. I told her you were stepping in to help since you were going to be here full time after we get married."

For some reason, the thought of Minnie being here to help Jack made Chelsea's back teeth ache. She ignored that to focus on the mess he had created. "So now I'm going to have to dump you in front of more than just my parents? I could have sworn we talked about keeping this low key." Anxiety crept into her voice, making it go higher than normal.

"I know, and I'm sorry. I didn't want to say anything, but then it just popped out when she kept pressing."

"Well, your popping out is going to make this so much more than it was." She had to think, yet her brain was giving her nothing. It was simply stuck on Minnie wanting to take Jack.

"Look, I said I was sorry, but don't you think I should be able to get something out of this arrangement, too? And it's not as if she's going to run around town telling people she wasn't able to get her claws into me. If anything, she'll keep it to herself and hope it falls apart so she can mend my broken heart."

"You're right. I know you're right, but this whole thing is getting completely out of hand. Maybe we should just call it off now."

Throughout the conversation he hadn't touched her. They stood on opposite sides of the foyer, both with arms crossed. She released her stance first. "You aren't getting anything out of this, Jack, I realize that. And if I can keep Minnie off your back for a little while, then I guess that's the least I can do. But you might want to start working up your defense now for when she wants to comfort you afterwards."

His hand clamped to the back of his neck. "Yeah, I thought about that, and I guess it's a risk I was willing to take so I could get rid of her for the moment."

"We'll figure something out. Don't worry about it." She crossed her fingers behind her back, hoping she was right. "I'm going to run that stuff over to my mother's and see if any grapevine news about this has gotten around town yet. My mom's the hub. She would know."

Taking the bag out of his hand, she ducked out the front door around him, trying to ignore the emotions churning up her stomach.

She spent the drive over to her mother's coming up with a way to ask for her mom's time without being overly needy, fighting her guilt for leaving Mazzy, and avoiding thoughts of being in Jack's arms. Not to mention dreading the news of their engagement storming through town. It didn't work. Winging the conversation with her mom was the only way to go. No matter how she fought the guilt, it was still there. And Jack looked and felt way too good to be shunted aside that easily.

When she entered the house, she was no closer to settling everything inside herself. She found her mother comforting a cranky Mazzy. Her little girl did not always wake up as happy and chipper as she was in front of company.

"Who's my lovely?" her mother was saying and stroking Mazzy's hair, the fine brown strands sticking out with static electricity from where she'd had the blanket wrapped around her head in sleep.

"I am." And the thumb went right into her mouth.

Leigh gently removed it, reminding her big girls did not suck their thumbs. Chelsea was afraid her child would burst into tears, but then Mazzy spotted her and the pout immediately went away.

Chelsea rushed over to her little girl's open arms, holding her close and knowing there was nothing more important in her world than this precious child who was everything to her.

"Did you just wake up?"

"Yep." She tried to sneak her thumb into her mouth again, but Chelsea took it out without a word.

"I think the knot fairy found you again," Chelsea said as she smoothed down the flyaway hair.

"She did. She did! She likes me. I hope the sock fairy will find me one day, too, so I can wear two different socks without worrying about making you mad."

Chelsea laughed, loving that Mazzy remembered both of the books she had bought for her at a signing last year. They were creative and fun and made Mazzy giggle. Chelsea would do anything for that sound.

"Why don't you go in to the potty and we'll see you in a minute, sweetie."

Mazzy dutifully got off the big-girl bed in the guest room and made a beeline to the restroom, singing to herself about the fairy that got her into trouble.

"What's up?" her mom said before Chelsea got a chance to open her mouth.

Nothing like being read before she'd had a chance to formulate how to make this sound like her mother's idea. Not that it would have worked, anyway, but it would have been nice if it were possible.

"You have that line between your eyebrows." Leigh said, standing up to smooth her forefinger along the crease on Chelsea's forehead. "You're on vacation and newly engaged. You shouldn't have a line like that."

"I don't have a line." She brushed her mom's hand away and put her own fingers on her flesh. There was no line. She refused for there to be a line. She could do this. All she had to do was inform her mother of the change of plans and hope to survive her sister. With any luck Belinda would see this was really just an extension of the job Chelsea had already agreed to do for her and let it go at that.

"You don't now. What's going on?"

"I, uh, am going to be helping Jack out with things."

"Of course you are, that's what your sister wanted you to do. You're filling in for Paige." She left to help Mazzy in the bathroom, dismissing the conversation.

Chelsea knew she could leave it at that and just

make a point to address everything with Jack behind closed doors. Then it would not be necessary to lie further. But her mom would hear from someone how she was running the inn with Jack. If Leigh heard it from Chelsea, then at least she could control how it came out.

She decided to get it out like ripping off a bandage, quick and with as little pain as possible.

"I'm going to step in for Adele for the next two days because she's sick," she said, raising her voice to be heard in the bathroom, "but most of my jobs will still have to do with the wedding. It's all the last-minute stuff Jack had lined Adele up to do to make sure the inn is perfect for Belinda's big day. I just need you to watch Mazzy a bit more than we had originally intended. I'm probably going to stay a little longer on Sunday, so it will be the next three nights." There. She'd said it and the sky hadn't fallen.

But a quick look at her mom's face showed her that while the end of the world might not be on the way, the hope there bloomed so high it would only make the crash harder when it was all done.

"That's wonderful! Your dad and I were just talking the other night about how once you come up here you could work right at the inn and spend more time with Mazzy and be a mom. I'm so excited for you! It's a shame you can't just stay and not go back to your apartment. Just transition right into your new life. And you know how I wanted my girl to spend the night while you were here anyway. This is perfect!" Leigh's face glowed as she clasped her hands to her chest.

"Yes, well, actually, I have to go home to pack stuff up and say my goodbyes. But for the moment, we're trying it out to see how it works. I wanted to do it without Mazzy for right now, so I can get a feel for things." The words burned on her tongue, and it was all she could do not to hang her head in shame at the pleasure radiating from Leigh.

"This is going to be so fantastic! But don't forget the main purpose right now is to get your sister hitched without a hitch while you have a real vacation. I know how you can overwork yourself." The look on Leigh's face was one Chelsea had seen before, one she understood. It said she was trying too hard.

"I'll be fine, Mom, as long as you don't mind spending a little more time with Mazzy. I don't expect it will be much more than I'm already doing." She'd already added a line to her own list, one that read "keep Belinda sane." With the hike tomorrow, she might have to leave that unchecked.

"I'm sure you'll be fine, honey, and it's probably not much more than what Belinda already has you doing anyway, right?" Her mother stared at her and cocked her head to the side. "I guess when I said you shouldn't have to do everything for everyone I probably should have realized the hypocrisy of that remark."

Chelsea blushed and ducked her chin, shrugging her shoulders. "It's not a big deal, and I volunteered."

"Only after you were pestered."

"I enjoy doing this kind of thing. I think it will be fun to help out at the inn and will probably be a more exciting job than the one I have back home." And that was true, though she did not let the thought take hold. She brought the plastic bags out from behind her back. "Here, Jack picked up some things for Mazzy to ease the transition."

Leigh laughed as Mazzy ran out of the bathroom. "That tricky devil." She handed Mazzy the loot and stood back as she tore through the bags and arranged the items out on the floor in front of her. Mazzy was busy before she drew her next breath, humming to herself and playing with the coloring books.

"Looks like they're a hit."

"Yeah." It seemed like he always knew what to do and how to do it.

"Okay, then. Enjoy yourself. And if Belinda says word one about this in a negative way, you send her to me. I'll take care of her," Leigh said. She turned to the coloring book where Mazzy was furiously scribbling with her tongue poking out of the side of her mouth in concentration. Her mother stroked a hand down Mazzy's hair in a way Chelsea remembered from her own childhood. "And maybe you can actually have some alone time while you're at it."

Leigh winked and chuckled when she said it, making Chelsea aware that while she didn't exactly say his name, her mom was implying that the alone time would be with the very hunky Jack. She tried hard not to groan.

Leigh's smug smile was not lost on Chelsea. Fortunately, she was paged by the new cell phone/walkie-talkie on her belt and had to hurry out without lying to her mother again. Being engaged meant she should want alone time with Jack. But she didn't. Hopefully taking on these other jobs would have her running so fast she'd have no time for Jack at all.

Or so she told herself even as the sound of Jack's voice over the walkie-talkie made tiny little shivers run down her stiff spine.

****

Jack heard the clatter of heels up the stairs and it brought him out of a problem he had been wrestling with after he'd paged Chelsea. With the phone against his ear, he signaled for her to wait just a second. He was trying his damnedest to sort out a glitch with the food supply company who was supposed to be shipping in the ingredients for the wedding feast. What on earth was he going to do if they couldn't give him the mozzarella balls in oil with cherry tomatoes, just as Belinda had requested? He didn't doubt Frank could come up with something, but it wouldn't be the same. Even with the way Belinda had already played havoc with other requests, he didn't think she'd be willing to entertain a change from his side of the desk.

Chelsea waited patiently in front of him, looking pretty in a crimson shirt with a square neckline allowing a hint of cleavage. It gathered beneath her breasts before flowing to her curvy hips. The sleeves stopped right below her elbows and the jeans fit her snugly. He listened with half an ear as the distributor continued to give him options and excuses, but his concentration was split by the way that denim hugged her thighs.

He shifted his focus to an innocuous picture of a landscape his mother had purchased at an auction two years ago. Now that the wedding was hours away, he'd have to put Chelsea even farther away from his mind. She was not staying, he knew that. His concentration had to be solely on getting this wedding to go off without a fault. He could not afford distractions in the form of a smooth expanse of skin that looked good enough to nuzzle.

By the time he'd hung up, he was back on track and firmly in owner-mode not man-mode. She was leaving, and he would have to soldier on after she was gone.

"That was the food supplier in New Jersey. They were supposed to make all your sister's cheese ball dreams come true. I have to go talk with Frank about alternatives. Do you mind manning the phone for a minute while I get my ears blistered?"

Her smile creased the corners of her eyes just enough to invite him to do the same thing.

"Surely Frank's not that bad."

"Ha! You haven't seen Frank in an herb rage. It is not pretty. Cheese isn't better."

"I could go talk with him, if you want. I've made the cheese ball thing from scratch, if we're talking about those mozzarella balls she wants."

Relief coursed through him before he could stop it. He couldn't send her into the lion's den. Could he? It would be wrong. Wouldn't it?

But she walked away before he could argue his way through not taking the easy road.

"You take calls, I'll be right back. Then whatever else you needed me for can be talked over."

She was gone without a backward glance. But he took a back-end glance and wasn't in any better shape than when he had tried to put that tantalizing neckline-framed skin out of his mind. Her curves fit into those jeans in a way he was sure they were designed for. Maybe this hadn't been such a good idea. At least when she was just a guest he could try to stay away from her when they weren't pretending to be engaged for the benefit of others. But he'd made a suggestion and a move in desperation, with Adele out of commission. He hadn't thought it all the way through. Now he would be with and around Chelsea much more than before.

Her words—"whatever else you need"—made him aware of how long it had been since he'd dated, much less slept with someone. That had to be put far away from even the back burner. Back in the refrigerator would be better.

He would have slapped himself in the head if he hadn't seen the kitchen door swing out and a very pleased Chelsea walk through it. He glanced at his watch just to make sure he hadn't fallen into some kind of fugue where hours had gone by without him knowing. Nope, it had been literally five minutes. He hadn't heard a single shout.

"Taken care of." She dusted her hands together and looked at him expectantly. "What's next, Boss?"

He couldn't help it, he got up with a laugh and then kissed her full on the mouth. Joy ran through his body at the contact. She was laughing, too, at first, and then it turned serious. He increased the pressure, running his hands over her shoulders, playing, just for a moment, with the frame of skin at the base of her neck. Their tongues danced and her sweet flavor sank into his skin. He could spend hours kissing her. Unfortunately, she stepped back and gave him a playful push.

"That's enough gratitude."

She thought that was gratitude? It had been so much more. Their first kiss should have gotten her out of his system, not infiltrated it to the extent that he couldn't think for wanting her over and over again.

But she held him off with an upheld hand. "Go check in with Frank just to make sure I didn't do him bodily harm."

The sparkle in her eyes was enough to bring him to his knees. He should go check on the guy for a heart attack. And to get himself out of temptation's way. "I'll be right back." He headed for the kitchen and was followed by the sound of her laughter.

"I promise he's not tied up and gagged in the other room."

He waved a hand to show he had heard her, but he still had to see for himself.

In the kitchen, he found Frank happily mixing a pot of corn chowder at the stove. Chicken stock boiled in another pot near his elbow.

"What the hell?"

The chuckle that greeted him did a whole lot of nothing for his bafflement.

"Hey, Boss Man. What can I do for you on this fine day?"

"You can tell me where the real Frank got to."

"I don't know what you're talking about. I'm making chicken and soup for dinner. Standing right here, happy as a clam in salt water."

"I don't believe you for a minute. Are you just saving up the tirade for me?"

His chef laughed, shaking his head. "There's not going to be a tirade unless you keep bugging me. Chelsea said she has a way to get the cheese things made, and I'm willing to listen to such a smart woman. Nothing wrong there."

Jack rocked back on his heels feeling a little helpless and a little bit angry. Chelsea had walked into his kitchen with demands and had not been eaten alive by his recalcitrant chef who normally liked to take

Adele's head and hand it back to her. It was why Jack had made an effort to handle the chef on his own for the most part.

"What's different here from with Adele?"

"Pah. Adele is a great girl, but Chelsea is a woman after my own heart. She walked in, let me know what was going to happen, and walked right back out. No nonsense, no questions, no wheedling. Actually, it felt like having a drill sergeant again, to be honest." The man smiled while whisking the soup in his big kettle.

"So I need to act like a drill sergeant to not get yelled at?" Jack made a note on his clipboard.

"Not going to happen, Boss Man. You try that shit on me and I'll have you cuffed to the plumbing before you could blink a second time."

Jack blinked twice now to see how fast that was.

"Just that fast," Frank said and laughed again. That was more laughter than Jack had heard in years from his chef at work. Unless the man was fleecing his cronies at poker, he never did much laughing around the inn while working. Jack had never been invited to the games, but he could always hear the swearing and laughter coming from the kitchen.

Now, Jack cleared his throat and judiciously changed the subject. "Are we good then with the menu still? I'm hoping we'll get no other calls with problems. But you know how things go in this business."

"I sure do, Boss Man, and I also know your extra help is going to go a long way toward smoothing things out."

Jack didn't believe that for his situation, though. Because as he came back into the living room to find Chelsea grinning impishly at him, he felt things crumple and knot inside himself.

****

The smile on Chelsea's face had been for Jack's benefit because inside she was having a hard time keeping all her emotions in check. She had never been kissed like that before in her whole entire life. It had made her go to jelly. When he left the room, she had melted, boneless, into the chair to her right. She could not handle being the wedding coordinator, the maid of honor, an assistant, and a mom, and still have time to fool around with a man who was not for her.

But, oh, how a part of her, a part hidden deep inside, wished she could.

She had jumped up from the chair as soon as the door opened. There was no way she was going to let him see how vulnerable she was. That kiss had been gratitude—that was all there was to it. Though she had never run a business of her own, she could imagine the pressures of making sure everything was perfect.

She had simply taken a situation that could have been a disaster and made it right.

He had thanked her and now they could move on.

But the way her lips still tingled told a different story.

He was not in her life plan. A relationship with any man was not in her life plan. And her home was over three hours away. So was the job promotion she would be given as soon as she got back. It was a culmination of all the things she had wanted to do for herself and for Mazzy. It would not be changed for lust. She had done that once and had ended up on the wrong side of the equation. This was an interlude and would not go any further. Perhaps if she continued to tell herself that, she would come to believe it.

All afternoon, Chelsea had busied herself with her increased list of duties. In fact, she'd been so busy she'd actually missed a call from Decadence, not her mother, and she should call them back. Was it really only almost dinner time? She felt like she'd been running for days.

"What's up?" she asked when Claudia answered the phone.

"Oh, hey, I just wanted to let you know the dresses are ready to be picked up whenever you get a chance. With the wedding Saturday, I wanted to let you know as soon as possible so you can fit it into your schedule, which I'm sure is busy."

Chelsea did a few mental gymnastics and said, "You know what? I'll be right over, because I do not want to have it be last-minute. Napkin rings are not all that important if there's no wedding dress to go before them. Are you open for a little while or were you just closing up?" She looked at her watch just to make sure the time on the phone had been right.

"Nah, we're open for a little longer, especially for a Moore."

"I'll be right over then." She hung up, then keyed up the walkie-talkie. "Jack?"

"Present." He sounded harried but it couldn't be helped.

"Is it okay if I take the inn van? I have to go pick up the dresses and I don't think they're going to fit in the back of my car."

"Sure. Keys are on a hook in the kitchen. See you when you get back."

And just like that, he gave over his van. She wasn't

supposed to compare him to Paul, but this was just one of those times where it was inevitable. Paul had been tight-fisted with the car keys well before they'd gotten married, but Chelsea had naively thought it had to do with her not being on his insurance. Instead, it turned out he had never let her drive their car, either, the one they'd bought with a bonus she'd received. They'd fought about it as they had about so many other things, but he'd never bent. And now Jack just told her to get the keys and go. It was a small thing, but it meant a lot to her.

Adjusting the seat to fit her shorter stature, she moved the mirrors to her liking and enjoyed the captain's chair instead of her low bucket seats. She would have driven one of these if she could have afforded it, even if she only had one child.

She left the radio tuned to the station it was on, because it was one of her favorites, and made her way over to Decadence. Walking in gave her such a sense of peace. They had really created something beautiful here. She'd heard that Claudia and Zoe's mom had started it long ago, and once Claudia and Zoe had joined her, they'd expanded it beyond the original dress shop. All she knew was that she loved it here and could spend all day hanging out. Especially since she really liked all three women who ran the shop. She hadn't yet met Claudia and Zoe's mom, but she was sure she'd love her now that she knew her daughters. They were warm, open, and friendly. When she'd talked with Paige the other day, she couldn't stop raving about them.

"Chelsea, hi!" May said, coming around the corner from the cake area with a chunk of something that looked decadent and chocolate. She handed it over before Chelsea had a chance to beg, then headed back the way she'd come and returned in a few seconds with another large chunk.

"Oh, thank you! I can't tell you how much I needed chocolate just now." She figured Jack would hold dinner for her, but with everything that still needed to be done it might be a while before she had a chance to eat.

"Everyone needs chocolate at least once a day, my dear." May smiled and sat down in her portion of the store on a brocade couch that welcomed Chelsea's tired body. "Enjoy. We can get the dresses in just a moment."

They both moaned as the first bite went down, and then they laughed.

"Claudia makes a mean cake," Chelsea said after licking her fingers.

"None meaner. And I hear we might get to make you a cake here in the future, if you'll let us. A dress, too. I have this great idea that would be perfect for your form and fit you like a dream. I made sketches, if you have time to look them over."

Chelsea's heart took a second to start beating again. How on earth did they know? How many people was she going to have to tell that it had all been a mistake and she and Jack didn't really love each other? And how fair was it that he was going to have to live in the fallout while she got to go back home as if it hadn't happened? What on earth was she going to tell Paige?

Tears leaked out of the corners of her eyes. She couldn't help it.

"Emergency girl meeting!" May called as she sat

next to Chelsea on the couch with an arm on her shoulder.

"This is not an emergency," Chelsea whispered fiercely, wiping her eyes with the napkin the cake had been on.

"Oh, yes, it is!" May said with way too much glee.

"What's up?" Claudia came sauntering into the room, and Zoe wasn't far behind.

"It's not an emergency. I'm so sorry for making May call you all together." She was a half breath away from bolting. What had made her break down in front of May when she hadn't said anything to her sister or Paige? Of course she couldn't really talk to Paige; Jack was her brother. She had just felt a little too overwhelmed, and now she had an emergency meeting with no agenda other than her own whining.

"Oh, we live for emergency girl meetings," Zoe said, settling in with a bag of cheese puffs and a soda.

Claudia took the bag from her and crunched a few cheese puffs too, smiling after she swallowed. "Emergency girl meetings are the lifeblood of this place, but I have to say this is our first guest emergency girl meeting."

"I really should go. I don't want to intrude."

Claudia wiped her hand on a paper towel May threw her and then laid her clean hand on Chelsea's forearm. "There's nothing wrong with new blood, and I'm all about women standing together. Don't you dare leave now that we have a bona fide emergency girl meeting. We haven't had a good one since Nate offered me eyewash when I was trying to flirt with him. He thought I had something in my eye, and I was just trying to bat my eyelashes at him."

Chelsea couldn't help but laugh, and she settled back into the chair with her hands in her hair. Maybe she should just have one cheese puff. Maybe it would make everything clear. Before she'd finished the thought, May shook the bag at her. "All things are possible with cheese puffs."

She blew out a breath and inhaled fake cheesy goodness.

"Now spill!" all three said at the same time.

She shouldn't have. She barely knew these women, and they weren't going to be able to help her. But the freedom of talking to people who weren't intimately involved with the situation was too tempting in her current state of mind. So she did, telling them all about everything from the initial lie to her mother to the ring on her finger and the tale she'd made up about the proposal. All of it came spilling out.

"So why can't you just tell him you don't want it to be fake anymore? That you want him for real?" Zoe asked.

"Well, for one, he doesn't love me, and I'm not going to rope him into something he doesn't want just because it's easier than admitting I lied to everyone."

"That's just crap," May said. "He was talking to my husband the other day and Brad was impressed without ever meeting you. He thought you must be about ten feet tall and made of pure awesomeness. Jack couldn't say enough good things about you."

That took a minute to process. "Well, we were kind of friends back in the day, and I highly doubt I've given him too much to complain about since we've been there."

May kicked up just one corner of her mouth. "It

wasn't just the praise. Brad got off the phone and said if Jack wasn't already in love with you he was well on his way down the road and it would be good to see him finally settle down with someone who was worth his time."

"He said that?"

"Cross my heart and hope to die."

Chelsea sank back farther into the couch. Did that mean anything? But he had Adele to do all those things and there was no need for him to talk to Brad about her, especially since he had only just spilled the beans today about the engagement. It was all so confusing.

"So what do I do? I want this to be real, I think, but we're talking about moving my whole life up here."

"What's so bad about that?" Claudia asked before popping another cheese puff in her mouth.

"Well, I've been trying to stay in the area there so that perhaps Mazzy's father will begin to take an interest in her. I don't want to move away if proximity would make that happen faster."

Claudia snorted. "Oh, honey, I have a story for you. I was pregnant at a young age and asked the guy to stay because we'd been together, and he left for college, instead. He came back just a month ago and Justin and his dad were so awkward with each other it was almost painful to watch. You have to go after what's best for you and Mazzy. If he hasn't come around in two years, he might never. Do you want to have lived your whole life in the shadow of hoping he might come around only to find out you've sacrificed everything for nothing?"

Chapter Nine

Chelsea sank back against the closed door to the drawing room after putting all the dresses in their protective bags on the long rolling rack. In a little over forty-eight hours this would all be over. The room had become her own and she would be sorry to leave it. She had yet to come up with the words or the courage to ask Jack if they could make this real. They could take a step back and she could move in with her mom for a little while, they could get to know each other all over again and see where it went. But she hadn't had the guts to say any of those things, and now time was running out.

Paige had called twice already, but Chelsea had texted her back saying she was busy and everything was fine. Paige had then left her a message.

With a groan, Chelsea listened to it.

"Chelsea Marie! You'd better call me back right now. This instant! Why on earth do I have to hear from one of the cleaning ladies that you are going to be my sister-in-law? What the hell is going on? If you don't call me I'm going to come over there… Okay, can't do that. But Plan B. I'll have someone kidnap you and drag you over here to tell me to my face what you and Jack have done. Call me! Now!"

"Finally!" Paige's voice burst through the phone without a hello.

"Hello to you, too."

"Don't you get snarky with me, young lady. I want to know what in the world is going on and I want to know now. This kind of stress is not good for me and the baby."

Chelsea covered her eyes with her hand, though of course Paige couldn't see her. "I'm sorry."

"For what, exactly?" Paige was trying to sound snotty, but Chelsea could hear the waver in her voice and felt terrible for making her cry. She couldn't imagine how awful it was for her friend to find out this kind of information from another person.

But what should she tell her? Chelsea opted for the truth at the last second.

"Look, I know you're probably angry, and rightly so."

Paige snorted.

"It's not what you think."

"So you didn't get engaged to my brother without telling me? You didn't fall in love with him months ago and not think to let me in on it? I can't tell you how much better that makes me feel. And after I hang up with you I am going to go after him with a vengeance. I told him to stay away from you."

"Now hold on a minute."

"I won't." Paige's tears could clearly be heard through the connection. "How could you do this to me? You're my oldest and best friend and I have to hear from Jessica Finkbinder that you're engaged to my brother. I think my jaw dropped off and I had to find it under the bed!"

Chelsea snickered, but tried to cover it with a cough. "If you'd let me talk for a sec I'll explain."

"Please do."

"It's a hoax. My mom was threatening me with a parade of eligible men while I was here, and I panicked and said Jack and I were engaged but she wasn't to tell anyone because we wanted to wait until after the wedding so we didn't steal Belinda's thunder."

"Go on."

"So then my mom spilled anyway and Belinda found out, and then your brother mentioned it to Millie, and it's all a mess."

"Ah-ha."

"What does that mean?"

"It means I didn't think it was real in the first place, but actually it would make sense in a weird way."

"It doesn't make any kind of sense."

"Yes, it does. Don't you remember when he had that crush on you at camp?"

"How did you know that? Even I didn't know that. How could you know?" Chelsea sat on the floor in front of the drawing room door in bewilderment. Why was she the only one who didn't seem to have known?

"Oh, come on! He tried to kiss you. I warned him off and said never again."

"You didn't."

"I did. You were too young and I was too short-sighted to see that I could have saved you from moving away."

"Oh, Paige." Chelsea rubbed her aching forehead. "I still would have moved, and if I hadn't I would never have had Mazzy. I can't imagine life without her."

"Well, there is that."

They sat in silence for a moment.

"So he really had a crush on me?"

"Oh, man, it was huge. I told him no way, you were my friend and totally off limits. Did he seem excited when you asked him to be fake engaged to you?"

"No, he was stunned and not exactly enthusiastic, but he did it for his sister's friend, and that's all."

Paige hummed. "I doubt that. So is that why you've been avoiding me?"

"I wasn't sure what to say and I didn't want to tip you off. I really hope you didn't tell your parents. There are already too many people who are going to think I'm an idiot."

"I did not tell my parents because it seemed hokey to me from the moment I heard. Are you sure your mom believes it?"

"Yes, absolutely. She's over the moon making plans for Mazzy and me to come home and live here again. She has dresses and themes and colors picked out for the wedding already." Chelsea sighed because she wanted all of that but knew she couldn't have it. She had a life back in Bettleton she couldn't just drop on a what-if.

"So make it real."

"No, Paige. I can't."

"Can't or won't?

"Won't, then. There's too much unknown, and I still have the promotion to go home to. So can I count on you to keep quiet until after Sunday when Jack and I will quietly break up?"

"I guess. But I still think it would be a great idea."

"So I'm no longer off limits?" she asked jokingly.

"You never really were. I just wanted to make sure that if he chose you it would last."

They chatted for a few more minutes and Paige promised again not to say another word about this. And then they hung up. Chelsea struggled up from the floor with a pounding headache and an overwhelming urge to go up to bed and fall fast asleep.

Resigning herself to the fact her time for sleep was far away, she texted her mom to check on Mazzy. Once she sat down at her desk, she plucked the folder for tomorrow out of the stacked desk boxes and flipped to the first page. Jack had taken care of the phone calls, but that still left arranging the gowns and accessories and making sure all the men's tuxedoes were ready and available. She had Jack to thank, too, for bringing down an old dress rack from the attic. They had played with the rack when they were younger. Back then they would take turns sitting on the long bottom shelf and rolling each other along the floor. So long ago.

Then she got down to work. Getting lost in the past was not going to make any red checks on this monstrous to-do list.

Her mom texted her back and let her know all was going well, just as she was finishing up one of the lists. Only three more things to go and then she would be able to call it a night.

She stretched and yawned once while she made copies of the seating chart for the reception on the handy-dandy scanner Adele had provided, and then it was time to close up shop. A knock on the door caused her to jump and straighten her shirt.

"Come in," she called out once she'd righted herself.

And then there was Jack, looking as fresh as he had this morning when he had dealt with Belinda again without losing his head. She, on the other hand, felt like twenty miles of rough road.

"I don't mean to disturb you, but I saw the light under the door and just wanted to make sure you hadn't fallen asleep with your head on the desk." His smile shouldn't have been devastating—this was her best friend's brother, for goodness' sake, shared kisses or not—but there was no denying it hit her low in the stomach. She should not be feeling these things for any man after the way Paul had left, much less for the guy she used to push in the mud during the first rain of every spring.

Swallowing hard, she forced herself to act normal even as her heart was doing a rumba in her chest. "No, I didn't fall asleep, but thanks for checking on me, and thanks, too, for taking Belinda in stride today." She had been at them again with demands for pink carnations instead of white, and three hundred roses' worth of rose petals to line her path to her groom. Together they had been able to talk Belinda down, and it had felt good to work with someone.

"She's a lot easier than some guests, so no worries." He laughed. "I had this one couple who would not walk on the carpet unless they heard the vacuum going outside the door no less than five minutes before they were ready to leave. They had even brought their own handheld unit for their room."

"You're just making that up to make me feel better."

"Boy Scout's honor."

"But you were never a Boy Scout."

"And I would never lie to you, so they kind of cancel each other out." He looked at his watch and then looked at her again. "So, if you'll notice, it is now way after five in the afternoon here in Pennsylvania, and I thought perhaps you'd like to celebrate getting through today. Shall we have a drink?"

She was tempted. That was not necessarily a good thing. Then again, she didn't have anyone to take care of tonight but herself. Only a very quiet set of rooms to return to, where she would probably not sleep because she was energized from the quiet and the things she had accomplished. Besides, what would a drink with an old friend hurt? She'd been so busy she hadn't even thought of their last kiss. He'd probably forgotten, too.

"You know you want to," he said, looking way too enticing leaning against the door.

"You used to say that when Paige and I were ten."

"I did, and you never could resist it."

She pretended to consider the offer, knowing she was going to take him up on it but not wanting to appear too eager. "I guess I could have one drink with you."

"Let's not put a limit on it before we even get started." He came farther into the room, moving doilies off a high-backed chair to take a seat. "How long has it been since you've had a night off? A real night without anything to worry about?"

The answer to that was "way too long," but she forced a smile on her face and shut down the laptop on her desk. "Let's go."

****

Having him follow her down the stairs was unnerving. She had never felt so aware of herself as a woman. And yet she did this all the time. Not the drinking wine with an old friend part. Certainly not the part where she had a night to herself. But the part where someone trailed behind her. It just felt different. She measured her steps and took in the scenery on the way, anything to not think about the fact Jack could be staring at any part of her and she would never know.

Finally they were in the speakeasy. He gestured for her to have a seat at the booth where she had sat last weekend with her family, laughing and joking. Right next to where he had kissed her the first time.

She wouldn't think about that, either, because it would get her nowhere, and fast.

"What'll it be?" he asked in a fake New York accent with a twinkle in his eye. "I got a good red or an excellent white for the lady's pleasure."

The way he said pleasure should not sound so good or set off so many butterflies in her stomach. She had to get herself under control or she would be a mess for the two days she had left.

"The white is fine."

"Coming right up." He poured the wine into two deep glasses, then corked the bottle back up and brought it with him. Setting a glass in front of her and the bottle on the table, he took the bench opposite her. "To old friends," he said, and lifted his glass in the air.

"Yes, old friends," she answered while clinking her glass to his and ignoring the way her beautiful ring sparkled in the low candlelight. The first sip went down smooth and so did the second. "This is good wine."

"And fine company." He folded his hands together on the old oak table between them and leaned forward. "Are you enjoying your stay so far?"

"Absolutely."

"Even with your sister breathing down your neck?"

She smiled. "Even then. Like I said before, I knew what I was getting into when I agreed to do this. I just hadn't thought she would still be going."

"Brides can be jumpy. Maybe not as jumpy as your sister, but still jumpy. Although, I have a feeling your sister has a lot in common with the Energizer Bunny. You're going to want to be prepared tomorrow. It might get worse, seeing as it's the day before the big day."

"Thanks so very much." Sarcasm dripped from her voice. "That's exactly the kind of pep talk I needed. She's already got herself all set up to go hiking, so that's no more concern of mine."

He reached across the table to squeeze her hand. "It's going to be fine, and then it will be done." He lifted his glass. "To getting the bride down the aisle without her running off. May I never have to do another wedding like this again."

"Here, here," she said, lifting her glass too. "I have a feeling Belinda's not going to be your worst bride ever, though. You'll have more experiences like her or worse if you want to be the wedding destination." Toying with the stem of her glass, she processed the information that someone else would be running those weddings. She wanted to ask if he ever intended to have a real engagement and a wife, but that might not be a question he wanted to answer, and she was having a nice time just chatting. She didn't want to ruin it.

"Yes, well, that's what I have Adele for."

"How long has she worked for you?" *And have you ever thought of her as anything more than an employee?* The question ran through her head before she could corral it. At least she hadn't asked it out loud.

"Adele's been here for about a year now. We're a

great team, and Frank, too. I might have to hire some additional people when more bookings come in. So far it hasn't been overwhelming, but I imagine if we book someone from out of state we might have to accommodate other out-of-town guests during the week before and after. This week has been good practice for us."

"That's true. It might just be your trial by fire." She took another sip of wine at the same time he did, then stared, fascinated by the way his Adam's apple moved with a sensuality she'd never associated with that particular part of the body.

"Fire I'm not worried about. It's the trial by bride that might take some doing." He leaned back against the corner of the booth and settled in. "Do you think she's going to get worse tomorrow? I'd like to be braced."

She propped her chin on her palm with her elbow resting on the table. "I would guess worse. That's why we put this system into place in advance. She's nervous, and she goes on whims when she's nervous. I think it will be okay with both of us working together, though." Working together. That was a novel concept for her since she had done everything alone for so long. But this felt comfortable since it was Jack, her old friend Jack.

"We'll figure it out then. Just tomorrow, and then we'll get her down the aisle Saturday and it will be done." He uncorked the bottle and topped off her glass. She hadn't realized she'd almost finished the first one.

But she felt mellow and had no responsibilities tonight. The world would not fall down around her ears just because she took a night off. "So tell me what you've been doing with yourself, Jack."

He peered at her over his first glass of wine that was still nearly filled to the rim. "Not nearly as much as you've been doing. Mazzy is an amazing little girl and she looks just like you. I couldn't believe it when I saw her running across the lawn. She has your hair and eyes and face."

"Or, as she likes to say, I have all of those things from her." Her lips curved at the memory of her daughter with her hands on her hips telling Jack that Chelsea looked like Mazzy, not the other way around.

"She is quite a pistol, but then so were you." Turning his glass around and around on the table, he said, "Truthfully, I haven't been doing much. I ended up going to college for a business degree and then helped out here while I got some experience. Then one day my dad comes to me with the keys in his hand and says it's all mine and good luck. They took off the next morning in their RV."

She could just see it—Jack coming back from school one day and getting the inn. She wanted to ask so many questions but settled for one that wouldn't put them in territory he might not want to tread. "Were you panicked?"

"Nah, running this inn is in my blood."

"But you had wanted to travel first and see the world." She remembered long afternoons down by the pond at the back of this huge property, swinging in the tire swings his dad had put up in the tree leaning over the water. She and Paige would swing for hours, until her rear end was numb, just talking about life and what they wanted out of it. They'd invite Jack to join in once in a while, since he had to watch them.

"Oh, I did travel. I went to Ireland and Turkey and Greece during the summers in college. But when it came down to it, I missed home. I missed my own backyard."

She sighed. She missed her own backyard, too. The one here that had a crepe myrtle in it that she and Belinda had played on as soon as it had bloomed. She missed the way the sun would come up over the mountains like a promise. And she missed seeing her family more than the once or twice a year they could get down to see her. But this life had been her decision and she had responsibilities in Bettleton now. No use wishing for anything else.

"Why the sigh?" He still lounged on the hard bench as if he had all the time in the world and nothing more to do with it than entertain her. And maybe he didn't. He had the inn, but that was where his responsibilities ended. He didn't have a young girl depending on him or rent to pay.

"It's nothing." She took another swallow of the wine and tried to swallow her tears with it.

"It is something, Chelsea. You know you can talk to me. You've always been able to talk to me."

Not always. She'd told him things when he'd catch her crying over some guy, but it was always Paige she talked to. She hadn't even had his email address when she found out she had to coordinate getting up here for the wedding. She'd had to get it from Paige.

Her silence must have made him rethink his statement. "You don't have to tell me anything, of course. I didn't mean to make it sound like you had to confide in me. Sorry." He sat up straight from his slouch and she wondered if she had wounded his ego.

But Jack had so little ego.

"No, really, don't get all pouty on me. I was just thinking about how we lost touch and that I was sorry to see it, though I didn't realize it at the time. We each had our own lives and we weren't constantly around each other anymore. I don't think I realized how much I missed that until I showed up this week."

"Well, of course you missed me. I'm the best."

He was, especially because he made her laugh. "Anyway, I can't change the past, but I'm doing a fair job of trying to not make the same mistakes in the future." Toying with the wine glass, she looked up at him from beneath her lashes. "I know you said you wouldn't bring Paul up again, but can I?"

"Yes, definitely. I told you I wouldn't mention him, but you certainly can if you want. I didn't want you to feel pressured, earlier."

"No pressure," she said, and squeezed his long fingers where they rested on the table. "It was just really hard to have him leave when I finally thought it might be my turn to go to college and I could get myself back on the track I had envisioned for myself." She rose from the bench, not able to sit still and stare at him while she laid her heart bare, but knowing he was one person who would listen to her and not tell any of her secrets.

"That seems reasonable."

"Not to Paul. He was involved with school and trying so hard to make good grades he often wasn't home, and when he was, he was sleeping. And then he graduated right before Mazzy's first birthday." She turned back toward him and took a sip of wine. She rested the bottom of the glass on her palm, pressing it into her flesh. "He was supposed to stay home with her in the evenings. He got a great job within two months and should have been home with Mazzy at night so I could go to school. But after a week, he said he was done and apparently not cut out to be a father." She laughed but it was a sad laugh. "One week and suddenly everything was different. I dropped out of my courses and took back all my hours at work. They were happy to have me back and I was happy to have something to pay the bills." She took one last swallow and put the glass down on the table. When he went to refill it, she put her hand over the top to stop him. "The rest is history, as the saying goes."

"Why didn't you move back here? Your mom would have helped you out with Mazzy and maybe you could have gone to school."

"I'm a naïve fool is why. I kept thinking that if Mazzy was accessible to Paul then he would miss her and come back to see her. But he never has. We have a life there, too. I can't rip her out of everything she knows to come running home to mommy with my tail tucked between my legs." She paced.

He stood, too, and stepped in front of her to cup her chin. "That's some pretty rough talk coming from someone whose mother adores her and her child and would welcome you back with open arms the second you said anything."

To avoid his all-seeing gaze, she dropped her head to his chest and felt something give a little inside when he wrapped his arms around her. "But I made my choices. Now I have to live with them."

"And you have, but if there's an easier way to do things, why not take it? Why not come home?"

Her mind a whirl, she looked up into his eyes and did the one thing she knew she shouldn't. It wouldn't change anything, wouldn't make anything better but could maybe make things worse. She did it anyway, laying her lips on his in a kiss that was laced with confusion and longing.

Chapter Ten

Jack savored the taste of her lips. Like fine wine with a slight hint of salt, they moved under his own like silk. With gentle prodding he was able to get her to open her mouth, and he swooped in.

Their tongues played across one another as he crushed her to him. Every part of her lined up with every part of him and had him yearning. This is what he had been craving. This was what had kept him awake last night. To hell with thinking he had any kind of point to make. The only point right now was that he wanted her and meant to have her.

He went from cupping the back of her head to cupping her rounded bottom with some interesting detours in between. Boosting her up onto the table next to them, he nudged her knees open so he could stand between them and press up against her heat. The skin of her back was tantalizing under her shirt, silky and soft and so very pliant as he pressed his fingers into her flesh. He made a slow trail from her waist band to her shoulders and then went back for another pass. The whole while he kept his hand at the base of her skull and her head tipped up toward his as he ravaged her mouth.

She made noises in the back of her throat and sighed into his mouth, driving him just that much crazier. What would she sound like if he had her under him? How good would they be together in bed when it was obvious they were good together out of it?

Her hands joined the game, running up and down his back, curving over his shoulders and then down. She made hasty work of getting his polo untucked and putting her hands on the skin of his stomach. Now he was the one groaning into her mouth. Her fingers were light, trailing what felt like butterfly wings over skin that was hot enough to scorch a field to dust.

He returned the favor and had the pleasure of finding out her bra was made of some kind of lacy fabric, her nipples pressing against the material to peak in the centers of his palms.

There would be no little girl for interruption this time. No monitor that came through loud and clear as Mazzy was waking up. All his staff were off doing other things. Even if they weren't they wouldn't come down here at this time of night.

He pressed up more firmly against her, loving the give of her thighs. Through his jeans and hers, he felt the heat of her and craved it like he had never craved anything before.

She tugged on his hair and brought his mouth more fully down on hers, taking his tongue in her mouth like it was a prisoner.

"Let's go upstairs," he said on a ragged breath. He would take her here, right on this table, but he wanted their first time to be something more than a quickie in the speakeasy. Backing away from her, he drew in her shaky exhale while taking her hand and helping her off the table.

"My legs aren't going to hold me," she said on a small laugh. "I'm not sure I can walk."

"Let me carry you then."

Even as she protested, he swung her up into his arms, enjoying the armful that was definitely all Chelsea.

She giggled like she used to when they were doing something they shouldn't. It was music to his ears. He kissed her lips to keep the contact going and hoped he made it all the way up to his room. They might have to only make it to her room, though, and then continue the journey to his suite later in the night. They had time.

"Put me down or you're going to break your back," she said as they reached the top of the stairs from the basement. As much as he would like to be a he-man, he had to admit that, though romantic, actually carrying someone up a full two flights of stairs might not be the smartest thing to do. He kissed her once more at the bottom of the second staircase, pressing her up against the banister. She felt so good everywhere. The need to get under those clothes to see how Chelsea had grown up overwhelmed him.

This was a culmination of every one of his recent fantasies, but it would be so much more because it had been such a long time coming.

They barely made it to her room. His shirt was out of his pants and up around his armpits as she kissed and licked him in places he hadn't known were erogenous. She fumbled with the doorknob behind her, laughing into his mouth when she couldn't get it open. Reaching beyond her, he did it himself and nearly fell into the room as she jumped up onto his hips and wrapped her legs around him.

"My God," he groaned, pulling her more fully against him, catching his hands underneath her and standing in the center of the room.

"Bed, bed, bed." She ran her fingers through his short hair over and over again, kissing him as if she wanted to devour him. And maybe she did.

Or at least he thought she did until her legs slid down from his hips and she turned her head aside as he tried to follow her down with his mouth.

Breathing heavily, he stared at her as she stared past his shoulder. She had a look in her eyes he couldn't decipher. Cupping her chin in his hand, he tried to get her to look up at him, but she yanked her head aside and took a step back.

"Did I do something wrong?" He turned to see what she was staring at and noticed the door to Mazzy's room was standing open. The little girl's bed was perfectly made up, with her blanket on the top in a place of pride.

"No."

The tears standing in her eyes didn't make him feel any better. "Then what is it? We were going hot and heavy and then you went cold on me."

A single tear fell. She lifted her hand to wipe it away but he did it for her, catching her hand in his and lifting it to his lips. "Tell me what's wrong."

"I can't do this." She took another step back but it felt like a mile.

"Why?" As far as he was concerned they were two consenting adults who had known each other forever. She must have feelings for him, since he knew she'd never just jump into bed with anyone who walked by. She had to know she meant a lot to him. He didn't see the problem.

Still not looking at him, she said, "I have Mazzy to

think about, and a job promotion when I get back home that will make our lives easier. I can't do this with you and then go back to my house as if nothing has happened. It's hard enough pretending to be engaged to you and knowing the fake life will never be real."

"I wasn't expecting you'd see it as nothing. I was hoping perhaps you'd stay." The words tripped off his tongue, stunning him. He hadn't meant to say them. Hadn't even let himself think them. But now they were out there, he felt right for the first time in a long time. Though he hadn't been looking to start a relationship, he found he wanted Chelsea more than he wanted peace.

Now she did look at him. "I've already changed my plans once for someone, and I can't do it again. I'm sorry, Jack. I really am. But I must have been out of my head to think this was a good idea." She walked stiffly over to Mazzy's room and took up the blanket off the bed. "I'm going to run this over to my mom's house. I'll be back later."

Before she could walk past him out the door, he took the blanket from her. "You just had two glasses of wine in a short time span. I only had a sip. If anyone is driving anywhere, it will be me." Then he left without looking at her. He didn't know if he could stand to see what was in her eyes, whether sadness or unrequited lust. Neither would have made it better.

In his car he banged his fist against the steering wheel. When would he learn that he was not enough?

****

Chelsea very quietly and very softly closed the door behind Jack as he left with her daughter's blanket. Mazzy would never be able to sleep without her wooby.

She should call her mother to warn her Jack was delivering it, since it was almost ten o'clock.

How had so much changed in so little time?

As soon as her mother answered she jumped right in. "Hey, I just wanted to let you know Jack's on his way over with Mazzy's blanket. I didn't think she'd be able to sleep without it, and I didn't want you to have to suffer all night with the crying."

"Hmmm."

"What's that supposed to mean?" Her heart fluttered in her throat.

There was silence for a moment, and then her mother said. "Oh, nothing, dear. I just find it curious that you sent Jack out at ten o'clock to deliver something to a little girl who is already sound asleep without it. She has a blanket here that she thought was extra cool. Since it smelled like the one at home she said it was fine. Which leads me to ask why Jack is the one delivering it and why you sound on the verge of tears."

"I'm not on the verge of tears," Chelsea said as she wiped moisture from her eyes. She had already cried, there was no verge about it. "Jack is bringing the blanket over because I had a couple of glasses of wine. I don't feel safe driving. He was sober, so there you go."

"Interesting. There I go, indeed."

"Why do you sound like you're trying to puzzle something out? There's nothing to puzzle out."

"Oh, nothing. So if I were to ask Jack why he's bringing the blanket over and why you aren't apparently on the verge of tears, he'd say the same thing?"

"Don't you dare ask him a single thing!"

"Even more interesting."

Her mom could be a bulldog when she wanted to be, which was definitely not what Chelsea needed right now. A whopper of a headache brewed behind her eyes. This conversation was not making it any better. "Look, please, don't say anything to him. We had a bit of a disagreement. I did drink two glasses of wine and he only had a few sips. I asked him to bring the blanket over because I really did not want you to have to deal with her crying if she woke up in the middle of the night and her new blanket was not good enough."

"Okay, honey, I believe you. I won't interfere. This time. But you know you can always come talk to me. In fact, why don't you plan on coming for breakfast tomorrow and we'll have some girl time while your dad takes Mazzy to the composting place down the road. He has her all excited about seeing mulch, and you and I can talk."

"I have too much to do with the wedding."

"That's ridiculous and you know it. It's going to be a wonderful, perfect evening. It will not fall apart because you aren't all over it every second of the day. This was supposed to be your vacation, too. Now say you'll come over for breakfast tomorrow or I will ask Jack what happened tonight."

Chelsea sighed. "Okay, okay, I'll be there, but you have to make the French toast the way I love it."

"Deal, honey. Now I'd better go, because it sounds like Mazzy's knight in shining armor has arrived with her prize."

Chelsea flipped the phone closed, then willed the rest of her tears to dry as she leaned her head against the back of the door Jack had walked out of. He had every right to be angry with her. Heck, she was angry at herself. But staring at Mazzy's room and knowing her child had to come first made it hard to abandon all her principles and just hop into bed, even if it was with someone she had known for years. It was wrong and stupid on so many levels. Perhaps it was just a hormonal thing. But now she was going to have to face him in the morning, and she had no idea how she was going to do that.

For tonight, though, she was going to crawl into bed, curl up, and rest knowing that she didn't have anyone to worry about except for herself.

****

Two hours later, Chelsea was still lying there and had counted every tile on the ceiling. She had tried sheep but they kept wandering away. She'd tried stars but they reminded her of the way she had felt when Jack had kissed her—and especially when he had lifted her in his strong arms and carried her up from the basement.

She had felt cherished. A feeling that had been absent for years, not since the earliest days of her relationship with Paul. When she found out she was pregnant she had been on the verge of leaving him. She'd known he wasn't the right person for her, but then the surprise and pleasure of Mazzy happened. Paul was the best pregnant daddy ever. He ran to the store at all hours for anything she even whispered about wanting. He gave her numerous back rubs and slept out on the couch with her when it got to the point where she was uncomfortable in bed. He was the one to set up the child birthing classes and he practiced the breathing techniques at home with her at his insistence. She had found her love for him again during those months.

But then something changed when they brought the baby home. It was as if the dream of a small child was wonderful but the reality too much to bear. At first she didn't blamed him. Mazzy had colic and cried constantly at the beginning. Heck, many nights Chelsea sat up crying with her. But that was what you did. That was what you did if you loved your child. And Paul just hadn't loved either of them. Or not enough.

Chelsea got up from the bed and went to curl up in the window seat overlooking the driveway. She probably wasn't going to get any sleep tonight anyway, so she might as well enjoy the view.

With her knees cradled to her chest, she rested her head on her legs and took in the brilliance of a country night in late summer. Every star shone, sparkling and dancing on a black velvet curtain. She'd opened her window twenty minutes ago thinking perhaps it was too hot in her room and that was why she couldn't sleep.

Now a soft breeze that smelled of fresh cut grass and turned earth wafted through her room.

Paul had liked the city and insisted that if her parents wanted to see their granddaughter they would have to come to them. Chelsea hadn't been on board with the idea, but she also didn't want to fight when there seemed to be so many other issues. Her parents had gladly come down to them—and stayed in a hotel because Paul thought they didn't have enough room to have guests.

And the rest was history she did not want to think about on a night as pretty as this. She had felt like a woman, a real woman, for a few minutes in Jack's arms. It wasn't worth losing his friendship over, but she had definitely lost her head for just a little while.

She sighed as she saw his car pull up the long driveway. Where had he been all this time? He'd dropped off Mazzy's blanket hours ago.

Unless he had gone for a drive. It was the answer to any dilemma when they were younger. When she'd had a fight with her mom, he and Paige would pick her up and they would blare the music and drive around the back country roads until she felt better. He'd done it for himself too, taking them along in case he wanted to talk or just have someone to share the misery with.

They had meant a lot to each other back then. She didn't want to lose him again now that she'd reconnected with him.

Before she could think better of it, she jumped up and threw on her lightweight robe. Pajama bottoms and a tank top would not be enough to cover her up after their kiss.

She flew down the stairs and into the kitchen in hopes of snagging him before he went upstairs for the night. Just as she opened the swinging door into the kitchen, he disappeared through the door to the back stairs.

"Jack," she said quietly, not wanting to scare him.

He paused with his hand on the door and stood there for a moment. Running his free hand over the back of his neck, he blew out an audible breath. When he turned around, there was a definite edge to his voice. "What can I do for you, Chelsea?"

Gone was the easy camaraderie from the beginning of her visit. Gone, too, was the passion in his eyes from a few hours ago. She pulled her robe more tightly around her. This was not going to be easy. But then, when was anything ever easy for her?

"Do you have a moment?"

"I always have time for a guest. We here at the Barton Inn live to serve." He turned and bowed, mocking her.

All right, then they were going to do this the hard way.

"Can we sit?" She gestured at the table in the center of the kitchen. The table where they used to do homework. She wondered if she peeked under the left edge if his name would still be carved there with Paige's and hers. That seemed a lifetime ago.

He took a seat across from her, letting her choose first. With his hands folded in front of him, he looked all business—his face set in that fake smile, an accommodating air all but reeking from him. She wanted to scream in frustration, but that would never get her anywhere.

"Can we drop the fakeness, please?"

"I'm not sure what you're talking about."

"Come on. This is me. Who do you think you're fooling?"

"I believe you've exceeded your questions for the night. Now, what can I do for you?" He looked at his watch, then flicked his eyes back up to hers. "It's late and I have a lot to do tomorrow to get ready for Saturday. Is something not right with your room? Did you not get your full complement of towels? I can certainly take care of that in a matter of moments."

She did scream, just a little, and muffled it with her hand. "Look, I'm not going to play this game with you."

"You seemed perfectly willing to play with me earlier." He drummed his fingers on the table, giving away his frustration with that one telltale sign.

"That's not fair, and you know it." She placed her hand over his drumming fingers and stilled them, willing him to look at her, really look at her.

And then he did, his eyes softening along with his mouth. He still didn't look happy, but he no longer looked like he had a rod for a spine, either. "That wasn't fair. I'm sorry."

She squeezed his hand and tried to sort out all the things running through her mind over the last few hours. The way she had come alive in his arms. The way he had made her feel cherished. The way he had made her forget everything for just a little while. The way she had run and why. She wasn't ready to share all this with him, but she could at least get some things out on the table.

"I'm the one who's sorry." She drew in a breath for courage before plunging on. "I'm not sure what happened, what came over me. I shouldn't have let it go so far, and yet I did."

"Why did you?" He seemed to honestly want to know, but she didn't have an honest answer she could give him without putting herself and her well-being into jeopardy.

"I don't know. It all felt so good, you felt so good. It's been a long time since I've even been hugged by someone of the opposite sex who isn't related to me, and I guess I simply went with it." She shrugged, and he squeezed her hand this time. "It was just too fast and too much all at one time. I'm sorry."

****

"So what are you saying?" Jack asked, catching her hand when she got up to pace.

"I don't know what I'm saying, to be honest." Chelsea's eyes were red-rimmed and her nose shiny, but she looked beautiful to him. "We haven't seen each other in years, only reconnected over email in the last month, and never spoke on the phone since graduating from high school, and all of a sudden we're about to get naked…"

Just those words sent him back into overdrive, but he ruthlessly shoved his want down. This was not the time. He was not ruled by hormones. "Okay." If this was a minefield then he'd better watch his toes.

She swiped at her cheek with the back of her wrist. "Okay? That's all you have to say? Don't you think it was too fast?"

"Um, yes?"

She laughed, though it sounded watery. "I'm simply saying we went from a kiss to bed in the blink of an eye. I have too many responsibilities and things to think about to have a fling. I can't throw that all away."

He hadn't been thinking "fling" when he was touching her, holding her against his body. He'd been thinking "finally." He guessed they were in two different places. He was not going to be the one to put himself on the line, though. He'd done it once and she had thought he was joking.

"Tell me you understand," she said. She touched the side of his face with gentle fingers. It was a hard-won battle not to turn his lips into her palm and kiss her delicate, pale skin.

"I understand."

"Now tell me you don't hate me."

"I could never hate you, Chelsea." He brushed some hair behind her ear. "Let's just get back to the point where we were friends. We'll forget this evening ever happened. It won't be a big deal." He'd steeled himself for the end. It was just coming sooner than he had thought. He'd never gotten a chance to convince her to stay. "We'll go back to the way it was and it won't be a big deal. It was an aberration anyway. Just curiosity, right? It'll be fine." And then he kissed her on her cheek and wished her a good night.

Once up in his room, he kicked a chair and then cursed as his toe throbbed. Curiosity his ass, he thought, grumbling. She had been into him, into their kiss, and it had had nothing to do with it being too long, he was sure of it.

The question now was what did he do? Did he try to convince her they were good together? That they could be so much more than email buddies? Or did he let her go one more time, knowing this would be the last time he could handle her walking away?

Without realizing it, he had held her up as the shining example of everything he wanted in a woman for so long. She was kind and good, sweet yet sexy. She'd had a heart of gold when they were younger and never let anyone feel left out. She was a caretaker, but now she had a lot more to take care of.

Would he only be adding to her burden if he pushed this? Or would he finally have a chance to show her it was okay for her to have help, too? That it was okay to share sometimes and that was the kind of thing that made every successful marriage he'd ever seen work?

Was it fair to ask her to have faith and change her

whole life again in the hopes they could make it work? He knew she cared for him. But did she love him the way he had come to realize he loved her?

Thinking about Chelsea, he also had to think about Mazzy. Was he ready to be a dad? Was he ready to raise a child? He dropped his head into his hands. He hadn't been thinking beyond the moment when he was kissing Chelsea, but now that he had time on his hands, too much time as he waited for the sun to rise, he did think.

Being a dad to Mazzy would be a commitment. He shook his head at the thought of Paul being able to walk away from both of them. Jack was already so attached to Mazzy he had no idea what he was going to do when she left with her mother.

Maybe having Mazzy stay at her grandmother's house was a better idea than he had thought. He'd meant it when he told Chelsea that the little girl could have the run of the house. But he hadn't taken into account how having her in every nook and cranny of the house would have made it that much harder to let her go when the time came. It was going to be excruciating to let Chelsea leave after the wedding, after seeing what a great team they made, after feeling her soft and supple in his arms. He could not compound that with thoughts of how much he had enjoyed high tea and having a shadow.

Blowing out a sigh, he rested his head against the cool window overlooking the back garden. Normally the sight soothed him, but tonight all he saw was Mazzy twirling around in the flower beds and Chelsea smiling that radiant smile down on her.

He cursed as he realized he loved both of them

more than he had ever loved anyone before. They brought light and life into his world—and he was going to have to let them go. He didn't want to compete with the new promotion Chelsea had waiting for her nor rip Mazzy from the life she had always known. He was not going to try to get her to change everything if she didn't feel the same for him.

Eventually he slept, but morning, facing Chelsea as if they were no more than friends and he hadn't felt her lips all over his chest, was not going to be easy. Knowing he loved her and her daughter but couldn't make them choose between their old life and him might just kill him before this was all done.

****

The next night, laughter filtered up from the speakeasy, but this time Jack did not go down to catch a glimpse of Chelsea. She had made it clear that anything with him was out of the question. They'd worked together during the day, running the vacuum cleaners, dusting and washing windows, but every time he'd tried to engage her she'd find something else, somewhere else, on her clipboard's to-do lists.

Once this wedding was over, she would return home and he probably wouldn't see her for another five to eight years. Mazzy would grow up and probably not remember they had played endless games on the floor in the library or that she had once called him Big Man and demanded kisses from him. Perhaps it was best this way.

He had the inn to think about, along with the prospect of more events booking up once this wedding went off without a hitch. Adele was feeling much better and back to her regular duties like the pro she was.

Frank was happily starting the preparations for the big meal Belinda wanted for her reception. Things had settled down with Belinda's requests. Jack figured he would recover once he waved goodbye to all the Moore women.

Then why did he feel like going caveman and toting Chelsea off to some secluded spot where he could try to talk some sense into her? And if that didn't work, he could always kiss her senseless.

Straightening up the library one last time, he turned down the lights, then closed the door to Chelsea's office. That room was hardly ever used. It would be a good space for something else. He didn't know what yet, but maybe he would turn it into a game room just to eradicate the memories of her sitting in there, doing her work with her hair twisted into a bun with a pencil sticking out the sides. He could get a couple of arcade games, maybe a big screen television and a game console or two.

He leaned back against the closed door knowing he probably wouldn't do it. Too much nature sat outside the front door to make this a place where kids stayed inside playing video games.

Maybe a pool table then, and a couple of dartboards so he and Dex could hang out here instead of going to a bar.

Whatever he decided, it would have to wait until she was gone. He tried to ignore the emptiness gnawing in his gut.

He wandered to the top of the stairs leading to the speakeasy, drawn to the distinct sound of Chelsea's laughter amidst the other women laughing. She had a contagious laugh. Just for a moment he could see her being a hostess here, working beside him as Mazzy grew up running around the yard out back and doing all the things he and Chelsea had done when they were younger. They could have a good life here. But he wasn't going to beg someone to stay.

The grandfather clock in the hall chimed eleven. He heard lots of footsteps on the stairs. He didn't want to get caught mooning at the landing like some lovesick kid wishing for one simple glimpse of the girl of his dreams.

He hid in the kitchen as all the women came out of the speakeasy and headed for the front door.

"Good night, everyone," he heard Chelsea call out to the others. "I'll see you all bright and early tomorrow morning! I'm going to go pour my sister into a bed here and then call Marcus to let him know she's spending the night after all."

Murmurs of assent and final goodbyes were called out, and then he heard the front door close.

Chelsea might need help getting her sister up those stairs. He popped out of the kitchen just as she was trying to lug Belinda up the first of twenty-two risers. Chelsea's sister was taller but with the same curvy build. Chelsea was never going to make it up without falling over, especially with the way Belinda was leaning on her.

"Let me take her."

Chelsea's head whipped around and her smile was filled with gratitude. "Oh, Jack, do you mind? I said I'd do it, but I'm afraid I bit off more than I can carry."

"It's not a problem at all. Good thing you already had Marcus bring over her stuff for tomorrow or you'd have a hell of a time getting her ready." He put his shoulder under Belinda's arm and his arm around her back. He'd drag her up the stairs, if need be. She wouldn't feel a thing in her condition.

"I guess she got a little carried away with the drinking game we were playing." Chelsea stroked her sister's hair back away from her forehead and kissed her on the temple. "She's so excited and nervous about tomorrow. I felt like that when I started having contractions with Mazzy."

"Why don't you grab a bucket from the linen closet in case her nervousness comes spilling out of her mouth?" He grunted as he hauled Belinda's dead weight up the stairs. Three steps up, Chelsea caught Belinda's other arm and they wrestled her to the top of the stairs together.

He left while Chelsea got Belinda ready for bed, but stayed outside the door in case she needed something. Belinda was a guest now, in any case, and it was his duty to make sure she was comfortable. But he drew the line at undressing guests. Unless that guest was Chelsea. That line of thought didn't bear thinking.

He leaned against the wall, listening to the quiet sounds of Chelsea soothing her sister while getting her tucked in for the night. He made a mental note to have some hair of the dog ready in the morning, along with the concoction his mother had made him drink the first time he had a hangover. It tasted like ash but it did the job. Belinda was getting married at three o'clock tomorrow afternoon. After tonight, she would need something if she was going to look perky and happy to be tying the knot.

The hall lights were dim when Chelsea stepped out of the room and pulled the door closed quietly behind her. He knew the exact moment she noticed him because her whole body went stiff.

****

"Jack," Chelsea said with her hand on her heart. "You nearly gave me a heart attack. Don't sneak up on a person like that." She said the words, but in truth her heart was racing from being near him again.

At her mother's today she had taken a long look in the mirror and then gone out to have a fun lunch with her mother and her daughter. But on the drive home, her mother's words and Jack's words had run over and over in her mind until they had sunk in like a mantra.

What was she waiting for? She had asked herself the question while she kissed Mazzy goodbye and was told to say hello to Big Man for her and to give him a kiss. She had asked herself again when she had caught a faint whiff of his cologne just as he rounded the corner into the dining room when she was trailing along behind him on the way to her temporary office. And she had asked it again when she was getting ready for the bachelorette party tonight, thinking about how nice it would be to get ready with Jack in the next room reading or watching television. He could tell her she looked nice or help her fasten the clasp of her necklace. All the little things she missed because she was alone.

Alone because she chose it. But she could unchoose it if she wished.

"I thought I'd wait around and see if you had everything under control," he said, not moving a muscle of that lithe, big body. The one that had pressed up against her as she gripped the banister behind her for balance last night.

"She's in bed and comfortable. I can't speak for the

morning, but we'll get her in shape."

"That's good then. I guess you'll be turning in for the night yourself. Big day tomorrow."

"Yep." What kind of inane conversation was this? But she hadn't been ready to face him yet. She'd wanted to wait until after the wedding and see what could be salvaged after they both got what they wanted—him the wedding of the season and her a happily married sister.

"I'll say goodnight then, and wish you sweet dreams." He turned to walk away, taking all the air in the hallway with him. It came out as his name from Chelsea's lips.

He turned at the top of the stairs to peer back at her. She couldn't read his expression in the dim lighting, but she knew what she wanted and would trust she hadn't killed his interest after she had told him no last night. She didn't have to wait until after the wedding. She didn't have to wait at all if she didn't want to.

Taking slow steps, she walked toward him. She was unsteady on her feet despite the fact she had not had a single drink this evening. He waited for her at the landing with his arms crossed, leaning against the railing.

"Did you need something?" he asked as she came closer and closer—one careful step at a time, testing out if this was what she really wanted.

"You," she answered, watching his eyes go big. She looped her arms around his neck and pulled his head down to hers. He hadn't uncrossed his arms yet, but she hoped he would soon. She wanted to feel those strong muscles around her, press up against his warmth and draw him in the way he had drawn her in last night.

It took him a moment to kiss her back. A moment in which she almost pulled away and fled to her room. But then he uncoiled like a huge tiger and snared her in his embrace.

He raced kisses over her face, not missing a single spot. Her earlobe got attention when he gently bit down. "Are you sure? Be very sure, Chelsea, because I don't know if I'll be able to stop this time."

"I'm absolutely positive, Jack," she breathed, trying to put her heart into her words.

Fortunately her bedroom wasn't far away. Ten steps. He backed her up with a hand in the back of her hair and one on her rear end until they were pressed up against the door.

"Do you want to take this upstairs?" he rasped.

He was probably thinking about how she had panicked last night when she'd seen Mazzy's bedroom and all the responsibilities it entailed. But she had come to terms with that. Her mother was right. Paul had never loved Mazzy even a fraction of how much Jack had fallen for her in the last handful of days. He had been more of a father in six days than Paul had been in four years. She trusted Jack. And Jack cared more for her than Paul ever had. It wasn't a contest to win but a cautionary tale. She'd thought long and hard about it all and knew what she wanted. And he was with her right now.

"I don't want to go anywhere else. I dreamed of you all last night in that big bed all by myself. That's where I want you."

"And what the lady wants, the lady gets," he said against her lips as he turned the doorknob behind her.

He followed her into the room, never letting go of her even as he tumbled her down onto the bed. His hands were busy and so was his mouth. She didn't want to be left behind, so she joined in the exploration.

His chest was smooth beneath his shirt except for the enticing trail of hair that dipped beneath the waistband of his pants. There was an awkward moment when they were trying to take off each other's shirts at the same time, but they laughed at it.

"Ladies first," he said, and whipped his own shirt off by tugging it over his head from the back of the neck. It was sexy and made her mouth water.

She wanted him all the way naked. Making quick work of his pants, she then just stared for a moment. "Tasmanian Devil boxers? Really?"

"If they offend you, you can always take them off." His smile was devilish and challenging, so she took him up on his implied dare.

Soon after, she was naked, too. Then the room was filled with only sighs of pleasure and moans of delight. He found places she didn't know she would find so ticklish or arousing. She found places that made him groan and sigh into her hair as he clutched her tight.

They made love to each other, and at the end Chelsea went over first as Jack had said ladies should. But she made sure she brought Jack yelling along with her. He called out her name at that final moment, making her cry out again.

Chapter Eleven

Sunlight speared through the sheer curtains covering the large window across from the bed in Chelsea's room. Jack woke up with an armful of lusciously curved woman and had a moment of disorientation until he realized it really hadn't been a figment of his imagination. He had made love to Chelsea Moore. Nothing before had ever compared or prepared him for the truth of actually making love to her. It was so vastly different from his time with anyone else.

He nuzzled Chelsea's neck, banishing previous lovers from the room and sneaking his hand down to her breasts to make sure they really were as perfect as he remembered from last night. Her eyes snapped open and she smiled at him before stretching like a cat.

"Mmmmm," she hummed. She traced a pattern over his heart, right where she had planted herself.

Someone banged on the door, breaking up the idyllic moment and the promise of perhaps a repeat in the daylight where he could take her all in with the sun glowing on her delicious body.

Chelsea's gaze shot to the clock on the nightstand. "Oh, my God," she whispered into his neck. "You have to hide. I should have been out of bed an hour ago."

"Chelsea," Belinda yelled through the door a second later. "Let's go! You should have woken me up an hour ago. We're running behind, and I have to get beautiful. Why did you let me sleep so late?"

"Please," Chelsea said in the same whisper. "Please go into the bathroom. If I don't open the door she might go looking for you to break the door down, or ask Adele for an extra key."

"Since we're engaged, don't you think she figures we're sleeping together?"

"It doesn't matter. Please go!"

He eased himself out of the bed, naked as when he got into the shower, and took some serious satisfaction in the fact she couldn't take her eyes off his body. He leaned in for a quick kiss, not quite what he had wanted, but it would have to be enough for now. On his way to the bathroom he scooped up his clothes from the floor.

"Chelsea!"

"I'm coming, Belinda. You're going to wake the freaking dead. Hold on a second."

He wasn't ashamed to admit he watched her throw on some clothes from a crack in the bathroom door. He only pulled the door shut when she made shooing motions to him.

He heard Chelsea open the door and then close it behind her. Their voices were muffled, so he knew they were in the hallway. It was safe for him to come out. Just in case, he got dressed first. He supposed he could pretend he was fixing her plumbing, or something equally owner-like, if they came barging back in, but it didn't happen. Waiting again until their conversation moved out of his hearing range, he came out of her room.

Unfortunately, he hadn't listened for extra

footsteps and came face to face with Adele.

"Looks good on you, Boss," she said as she walked by and made her way down the stairs laughing.

What looked good on him? Making love? Could she tell? But then he realized his shirt was on inside out and backwards. He sighed.

****

"Are you ready?" It was the last question Chelsea had and her last duty as official wedding planner.

Belinda looked resplendent in her white gown. The waterfall skirt fell to the floor in gentle folds decorated with clusters of stars in crystal. Twitching the hem, Chelsea tried to ignore the emerald flashing at her. She had decisions to make that needed all her concentration. Moments before her sister's wedding was not the time.

"I'm so excited." Belinda stared at herself in the mirror, her eyes misting.

"There will be no crying until after the ceremony." Chelsea said with a smile. "We don't want to ruin your makeup."

"No, I don't think I'm going to cry at all. Can you believe this has been nine years in the making? And it's all come together so beautifully, Chelsea. Thank you for putting up with my crap this week."

"Oh, it wasn't so bad."

Belinda nudged her with a bare shoulder. "I'm sure that's not what you were saying yesterday morning when I went for that hike. I was just so nervous, but now that it's here, I'm ready."

"You look beautiful, and this will be the best day so far. The rest will be gravy as a married woman."

"And then it's going to be your turn." Belinda hugged her with enthusiasm.

Chelsea was thankful she was turned away from the mirror so no one could see the tears standing in her own eyes. Most would probably mistake them for tears of joy for her sister, but she knew in her heart that they weren't. Or at least not completely.

After waking up with Jack this morning, she had been thankful for the rush of the morning. It hadn't allowed her time to think too much about what she had done and how she had let her heart open for him last night along with her body.

Now that everything was almost done, though, she wasn't going to be able to put off the heartache forever. If nothing else, at least she had the memories of last night to hold her over. Perhaps she and Jack would be better about keeping in contact after she left. She'd dreamed of living here, growing here, her daughter thriving here, but then she'd looked at her calendar this morning and realized two days from now she had her promotion meeting. The futility of those dreams came crashing down around her.

She had a life back in Bettleton, one that fulfilled her even if it wasn't the same as being home. One she had been happy with until she'd come back here. She would be happy, again. She might just have to work a little harder at it. But she'd never shied away from hard work. It was what had gotten her where she was. As much as she had loved being with Jack last night she still didn't know for absolute sure if uprooting herself and her child was in anyone's best interest. Maybe she was being selfish. Waiting around for Paul was really no longer the answer, but she'd been doing it for so long she didn't know if one night in Jack's arms should change everything she'd built for herself up until this point.

A knock on the door saved her from deeper thoughts.

"Music's started," Jack said through the wood. His voice sent a shiver up her spine. He'd whispered sweet everythings in her ear last night while he'd been inside her, making her soar in a way she never had before.

She wished, for just a brief moment, that she could reconcile her feelings. That she could move past this fear of failure. But he hadn't spoken of love, they hadn't made any promises, and even if they had, she wasn't ready to give up everything she had worked for on the hope that things would work out this time for her.

"Coming!" she called back and gave Belinda a final hug. Today was not about Chelsea and her issues. It was about Belinda and Marcus and their love for each other. Today would be beautiful. When it was all done, she might have to hand the ring back to Jack and never think about the fact that some other lucky woman might wear it one day.

****

Jack pulled at the collar of his tux as things wound down. The wedding had gone off without a single hiccup. Belinda and Marcus had promised their forevers, the food was great, the dancing funny and sometimes poignant. Hugh Moore had twirled Belinda out on the floor with a tear in his eye. He'd swiped at that tear when Marcus cut in on their dance.

Jack hadn't been able to help himself when he sought out Mazzy a moment later wondering if he would be able to give her away someday.

The engagement might have been fake, but what he

felt for Chelsea was real. He'd come to the decision that he couldn't let her leave without at least trying to convince her to stay. They didn't have to remain engaged if she didn't want to, but he wanted a chance to see if that was where they would have ended up if she lived here.

Once all the guests were gone and Belinda and Marcus were shut up in the honeymoon suite, he was going to entice Chelsea into a moonlit walk and propose for real. If not with a ring then he would propose that they give this thing a try. They were good together, in and out of bed. Maybe that would be enough to make her think about moving up here permanently. They could take their time getting to know each other if that made her feel better, but he already knew where his heart belonged.

"Thanks, Mom. I'll see you in an hour," Chelsea said, hugging her mother. The older woman had Mazzy on her hip as she kissed Chelsea on the cheek.

What was going on? He'd thought they would have the evening together.

Chelsea leaned back against the closed door with her eyes closed and a frown marring her brow. What was going on in that busy mind of hers?

No time like the present to find out.

"Everything went really well," he said, then watched as her body stiffened. He hoped that didn't mean what he was thinking.

"Yes, it did." She slid her eyes to the side, not looking at him but to a point over his shoulder.

"So what time are you leaving tomorrow morning?" And how could he convince her not to go at all? He thrust his hands into his pockets. He was getting some distinct hands-off signals from her. What had changed between this morning and now?

"Actually, I think we're going to leave tonight instead. Things wrapped up sooner than I had hoped, and Mazzy and I could do with a few extra hours at home. Plus, it will be nice to sleep in my own bed. Not that I haven't loved sleeping here…" She trailed off with a blush.

He fidgeted with the change in his pocket.

"Anyway, I'm going to pick up Mazzy once I have all my things packed here, and then we'll head out. It's been great here and I appreciate the hospitality, Jack. It's been a great week, but it's time to get home."

She made to walk past him and he grabbed for her left hand, feeling the emerald ring dig into the palm of his hand. "And that's it? You're just going to go? Even after last night?"

"Yes, and I should get started packing if I want to get to my mother's on time." She broke his grip and walked away, taking his heart with her.

Stunned, he let her leave. Once he got his wits back he took two steps to follow her. But he blew out a breath with his foot on the first step to the second floor. He wasn't going to chase after her. He knew when to let go, and this was one of those times. She'd made up her mind and there was nothing he could do to change it. This was supposed to be temporary, anyway, and it was his own fault for making it more than he should have.

He went to the kitchen to see if there was any booze left. He couldn't watch her walk out the door with his heart dragging along behind her.

"Frank, I need a drink. Tell me there's something left," he said, entering the chef's domain. He'd take cooking sherry at this point. He did not want to go down into the speakeasy where he and Chelsea had made memories that would haunt him.

Two heads popped up at his words. Belinda and Frank looked guilty as hell. The bottom dropped out of Jack's stomach. What on earth could Belinda need when she should have been in the honeymoon suite getting wrapped up in her new husband?

"Um, hello," he said.

"Jack." Belinda rose from the table in a soft pair of yoga pants and a t-shirt that said The New Mrs. Rushland. Her previously shellacked hair was piled in a messy bun on top of her head and her face clear of makeup. She looked so much like her sister it made his chest hurt.

"Guilty as charged. What can I do for you?" Please don't let it be one of those things that needed to be passed by Chelsea. The wedding was over.

"It's what I can do for you."

"And what's that?" He shouldn't have asked, he realized when he saw the gleam in her eye.

"You and Chelsea for real."

He swallowed his tongue for a moment, then stuttered a lie. "We are real. Why do I need your help with that?" He ignored the way Frank shook his head at him from behind Belinda's shoulder. But it should have warned him.

"Don't bullshit me. I've known since the second day that it wasn't true. Mom knows it, too. But we kept hoping that this week with the two of you together would make Chelsea see things she's never taken notice of before. Now she's leaving early, and I'm thinking you didn't convince her enough."

Dropping into a chair at the kitchen table, he massaged his forehead. So the ruse was up and had been for days. Chelsea was not going to be happy. Maybe he could convince Belinda and her mother never to mention it to Chelsea. But Belinda beat him to it.

"Look, we're not going to tell Chelsea that we knew, but I want this to be real. The two of you are good together. She's been happier this last week than she has been in years. Selfishly, we want her back in the area, but we also want Mazzy here, and we want them both happy. You're good for them. Good *with* both of them. They need you and I bet you need them. Now, Frank and I have been talking, and we have a plan."

"A plan is not going to help. She wants to go home. What are you going to do? Pop one of her tires so she can't leave?"

Frank's guilty face actually made Jack laugh. "Come on. She's a grown woman. She can make her own decisions. I'm not going to force her to stay. And if we do something underhanded like that, she's going to miss out on her promotion. It means everything to her."

Belinda got up to pace. "It doesn't mean everything to her. It means financial security, yes, but it also means more hours, more time away from Mazzy, less time to be a mother to her and less time to come up here and visit. Paul ruined a lot of things when he left, and Chelsea's confidence and trust are two of the casualties. She loves you, Jack, I know it. You have to tell her you love her and make her stay."

"What if she doesn't love me?"

"That's just stupid, Boss Man. 'Course she loves

you. Don't think Adele didn't tell me about you sneaking out of Chelsea's room this morning. After a week I know that lady, and she has strong feelings for you. And you have them for her and that little girl. Go fight for her."

"But what if she doesn't want to be fought for? What if you're wrong?"

Belinda smacked him in the back of the head. "I'm never wrong, even if you wouldn't let me have red and green lettuce at my wedding. She wants to be fought for. She wants someone who wants her, too, not just a free ticket to college and then no responsibility. Go get her, or so help me God I will make your life miserable."

Jack laughed to release the tension in his chest and gut. "You don't think this last week hasn't already been hell from you?"

"But it brought Chelsea back. Why do you think I had my wedding here in the first place and made her stay here instead of camping out in Mom's guest bedroom?"

"You've been planning this all along?"

"And you fell right in, big boy. Now go get her before she gets into her car and I have to shoot an arrow in one of her tires."

****

Chelsea gave her report to Paige over the cell phone as she packed her things. Mazzy was not going to be happy about leaving early to go home, but it was time. She couldn't stay here another night. During the reception, Belinda had insisted Chelsea and Jack dance together as the people who made this all possible. Being in his arms had been heaven and a little bit of hell. His strong embrace surrounded her, making her feel cherished, something that had been missing for so long it made her heart hurt. It had drawn her tighter than the wires on a brand-new piano. It was better to cut and run now. There was nothing else to do here but make more memories that she might not be able to recover from.

"Yes, Paige, I'm going home. It wasn't a disaster and everyone lived at the end. But I'm ready to get back to my normal life."

"That's what your words are saying, but your tone is saying something totally different. Now, you know you can't lie to Paige, so don't go there. I could have sworn you were really falling for my brother the last time we talked, when you were trying to convince me this was all a lie."

"It was a lie. It's not something I wanted." That was more a lie than anything else she'd said this week. "We can talk about this when I get back. I just want to leave and forget all about this."

"So it really was fake. I had hoped for something else, but I guess you have to do what you have to do. Was he really that horrible? Should I come beat him up? I'm sorry I put you in this position by not being able to do my job."

"Oh, no, that wasn't a problem at all. In fact, I had a lot of fun with all the lists and stuff. I learned you are the master organizer and I am not nearly as organized as I thought I was. But it all came together at the end and was wonderful except for that part where the bride tried to change everything and was a pain in the rear end." This was agony and she just wanted to be done and home where she could kick herself for her stupidity in peace and quiet.

"So if that wasn't the bad part, then what was?"

Paige asked.

"We'll talk when I get home. I can't do this right now."

"Or you'll cry? I can hear it in your voice."

"Yes, all right? I'll cry if I talk about the other part right now, and I don't want to do that."

"Well, then be prepared to talk for a long time when you get home. I have tons of time and you don't go to work until Monday. We'll make a night of it and talk on the phone."

"Deal. Now I have to get my car loaded up so I can start the drive. I have a feeling Mazzy is not going to be happy about leaving her Grammylove and Poppydove." Chelsea tucked more clothes into her suitcase.

"Good luck, then. And be safe."

After closing her phone, Chelsea leaned her head against one of the cornerposts of the bed. Some pretty amazing things had happened in this room, the way Jack had loved her not the least of them. But she had to go back to what she knew, what she had worked for. She knew in her heart things with Jack wouldn't work in the long run. She couldn't trust that they would. She couldn't put everything she had on the line.

And she would not put Mazzy through that a second time. Especially when she would understand, at this age, that someone who had loved her no longer did.

Chelsea threw the last few things into her suitcase and zipped it up. Mazzy's room had been cleaned out yesterday. There was nothing else to do. Nothing to hold her here. She had packed up all the stuff from her office this morning to avoid Jack. A part of her had thought maybe Jack would come in and they could talk, but he hadn't.

Now she was planning on leaving without saying goodbye. It wouldn't matter, anyway. She took the ring off and laid it on the dresser, not sure she would make it through handing it back without crying.

Dropping her bag to the floor, she popped up the handle and set it on its wheels, ready to roll out. But when she looked up, there was Jack blocking the doorway.

"We need to talk," he said.

"No, Mazzy is waiting for me, and so is my mom. I have to get going." She walked purposefully forward, fully intending to run him down if she had to. But when it came to the last second, she couldn't do it. She backed up and said, "Please." Her voice was pathetically weak, but she was on the verge of tears and she couldn't help it.

He moved, but only to close the door behind him and lock it from the inside. "We have to talk."

Now the tears spilled and she felt like a fool. She would have liked to keep some of her dignity intact, but apparently that was not in his plan. What she wanted didn't really matter. "Fine. Talk."

"I don't know what happened since this morning, but I feel like something broke between us and I didn't see it coming."

"I did. We would have never worked out, so I'm leaving. Now, if that's all, then I need to go. Mazzy is waiting for me."

"Actually, I called your mom and told her that you'd be a little late coming to pick her up."

"So then I'll just be a little earlier than you told her. Now please move." Because she was going to crack in about two seconds and would not, could not, do it in front of him.

"No."

"The ring is already on the dresser. It's over, Jack. Thanks for being such a good sport about being my fake fiancé for the week, but it's time to go now."

He stepped forward and caged her arms in his hands. "Look at me, Chelsea."

"I don't want to." She'd rather have her eyes poked out with a skewer than show him the hot tears burning her eyes. This was supposed to have been a fun something to get her out of having the week of bachelors. It was her own fault that she had let herself be drawn into something that was never real.

"Please."

"No. Now let me go so I can leave." She was dying right here and now.

"But I can't let you go." Tugging her over to the window seat, he sat and pulled her to stand between his legs. "I can't let you go now that I've finally found you again."

"I was never lost."

"I thought you were lost to me, and that was worse. Now we have a chance and I'm begging you not to throw it away because I was stupid. I don't want to have to live with the regret that I ruined it all when I finally had a chance with you. I love you, Chelsea, and I want you to stay. Please don't leave."

She was pretty sure her heart stopped in her chest and then began beating double time. "You love me?"

"I did for years, but that was nothing compared to how I've fallen in love with you over the past week. Before, it was like wanting something I never had or could have. But being with you this week has shown me who you really are, and I am deeply in love with that person. I want to be smart enough to keep you this time, Chelsea."

"But..."

"No buts. Tell me you love me, too. Tell me you'll stay, and we'll figure things out together. Even if you don't want to live here at first, I'll take you any way I can get you. Mazzy, too. I can't bear to see you leave. I can't bear the thought of not seeing that little girl grow up. To be a part of her growing up. To listen to her and influence her. I'm asking you to marry me and be with me always. You and Mazzy. If you want to go back to Bettleton, I'll go with you once I get Adele trained on running this monstrosity herself. She'd probably love the power."

"I..."

"I talked to Frank just now, after he slapped me in the head, and what he said made sense. We're good together. I need you. I need Mazzy. I'm going to have a hole the size of Antarctica in my chest if you go without knowing how I feel. I won't ask you to give up everything. I won't ask you to change it all for me. I just want you to include me. Make room for me in your life and I'll be there."

She put her hands to his chest and held him back for a moment. "Will you let me get a word in edgewise?"

"Not unless that word is yes." He said the words with a quirky smile but she could see the worry behind his eyes, feel it in his hands gripping her forearms.

She let her gaze trace the shape of his face and the way his hair fell along his brow. His face was burned into her brain in so many different variations—little boy chubby to gawky teenager to this man who stood in front of her laying his heart on the line. She could choose to walk away from this or she could choose to share herself with him in a way she hadn't with anyone. To trust him with her heart and her daughter's heart. What Claudia had said at the shop rang in her head. Did she want to sacrifice everything for something that would never happen? Was she going to let her doubts and insecurities keep her from making a loving life with someone who wanted her? All of her?

For the first time in a long time it was her choice, and she had to make the right one. Not the one based on other people's expectations or needs. Not based on what would make other people happy, but what would ultimately make her happy. She just had to let her past go and move beyond it. Or risk losing the one chance she had to make herself happy.

"I'm scared. What if we can't make it work? I know you said you've loved me for years, but what if I'm not all you think I'm cracked up to be?" she finally said, looking him dead in the eyes and not flinching at the admission.

He hugged her hard, dragging her into his arms. "I know you are. We've had this week together and you're everything I knew you were plus interesting facets I didn't know about. I want you to dance around the house and make additions where you see fit. I want to sit across the table from you with Mazzy asking for Big Man kisses and tromping me at Candyland. I want to teach her to ride a bike and take long walks with you." He kissed her on the temple. "With you it's all possible. I want to share with you. It's natural now to seek you out, to have you be my best friend, my soul mate, my everything. I can't tell you it's all going to be roses and rainbows, but I promise I will never let you down and I will always love you. Now tell me you love me, too."

Her brain short-circuited as she stood staring down at him. How could he not think that was rainbows and roses? It was everything and so much more than she had ever hoped for. More than she had ever allowed herself to hope for.

"Oh, Jack, I do. I do love you!" She sought his mouth for a kiss, one that curled her toes. "I want a life with you. Here, right here. We are not leaving when I finally get to live in the house I've always loved, with the man I should have known I would love, all those years ago."

He smoothed her hair back. "Mazzy is precious and the world would be far less bright without her. Everything happens in the right time. Like your sister's wedding. And now us. As long as the rest of your days are spent with me, that's all that matters."

"It is." And with his next kiss, she let all her fears slide away. He loved her. She loved him. And they both loved Mazzy. Their life together might have some bumps, but she was willing to weather anything with Jack, the man who had her heart firmly in his grasp.

Mazzy was going to be thrilled.

"We should go get Mazzy and tell everyone the news that I'm going to stay."

"Not yet," he said, as he started inching up the hem of her shirt. "I told your mom you were going to be busy for a little while tonight and she could keep Mazzy overnight. She said she hoped I was finally going to really make an honest woman out of you instead of trying to pull a fast one with a fake engagement."

"Oh, God. They knew?"

"Yep, according to Belinda, they figured it out the second day. But they played along, hoping we would figure stuff out on our own before the week was up. Belinda was downstairs with Frank when I went in to get a drink, and she was actually the one who slapped me in the head, not Frank. I wasn't going to tell you, but I want only truth between us."

"So we pretended for an entire week for nothing?"

"I wasn't pretending." His eyes smiled at her as his mouth descended for another kiss.

"I kept fighting how real this all felt. I wanted so badly to be with you, but I couldn't let go of the hurt Paul caused. And I didn't want to trust that things would be different with you, even though I knew they would be, saw they would be by the way you were with Mazzy and with me."

He captured the hand that had worn his ring all week. Her finger had felt naked the second she'd taken it off. Placing a kiss on her ring finger, he stroked her hair with his other hand. "It will be different this time for you. You can do whatever you want. If you want to go to college that will be fine with me. Registration is running right now for the community college, if you're interested."

"No, I'm right where I need to be. You're right, everything happens for a reason, and I know I want to be right here with you at the inn. I have experience now, if you want my resume."

He laughed as she meant him to. "No, I know you're qualified. If we can survive your sister, we can survive anything. Let me know if you change your mind about the college. It's an open-ended offer. This one's not, though."

Chelsea was waltzed over to the dresser and then Jack was on one knee in front of her with the emerald ring on his palm. It wasn't the gazebo with twinkling lights and a light breeze, but it was perfect. "Chelsea Moore, would you do me the honor of becoming my wife? I don't think I have to ask your dad, since he already gave us his blessing even if he thought it was fake. I don't want to live without either you or Mazzy. I want to make more children with you. We could have a whole passel running around, and we'll make the speakeasy our hideaway when things get crazy. I'll kiss you there like it was our first time again and again and again."

"Yes, Jack. Yes." And the tears came, but these were tears of joy.

He rose to his feet, caught the first tear on his fingertip and kissed the rest away as he slipped the emerald back on her finger. It fit as it had the first time, like it belonged there. And it did.

"Now that you've said the first thing I wanted to hear, let's see if I can make you say the next thing on my list of things I like to hear."

"What's that?"

"How about my name while I'm making you mine all over again?" His cheeky smile melted her insides to the consistency of hot chocolate.

She gasped, both from his audacity and from what his hands were doing to her. There would be plenty of time to be embarrassed in front of her mom later. Right now she wanted to concentrate on Jack and how good he made her feel, how loved.

"Tell me I haven't left you speechless. Not my

Chelsea Moore."

"No, but once we work on your list of things you like to hear, I have a few of my own."

****

The car ride over to Chelsea's parents' house the next morning was filled with plans and her stealing kisses every time they stopped at a red light. She wanted to tell Mazzy they were staying, and she couldn't wait another moment. She was so happy Jack had persuaded her to take the time to see if he would say the things she wanted to hear. And he'd said them all, plus some she hadn't realized she craved.

With their hands entwined on the gearshift, Chelsea couldn't believe her good luck in finding this one man a second time. Life would be full now of so many things, things she hadn't dared hope for. She was going to call her boss first thing tomorrow morning and let her know she wouldn't be coming back. There was another woman in Chelsea's department who would be perfect for the promotion Chelsea was giving up. Maybe she should have been more upset about letting the job go, but not with Jack and the inn to look forward to.

Jack made a right turn when he should have made a left. She opened her mouth to tell him he'd gone the wrong way, but almost immediately they pulled up in front a small cottage with a variety of bikes in the front yard.

He jumped out of the car, then came around to open her door. She could get used to this without a single problem.

An older woman answered his knock at the front door of the house.

"So you did come back for it. I thought you looked sad to leave it behind the other day, so I put it aside, just in case. Go ahead and take it."

"What about the other thing we talked about?" he asked, sounding cryptic.

"Ah, yep, I have that, too. You sure you want it now?"

"Yes, I'm positive."

"Okey dokey. Be right back. Why don't you load up the bike, and I'll just be a sec." She left the door wide open as she disappeared into the depths of the house.

Chelsea stood transfixed as Jack checked out a small bike with a banana seat and training wheels. It had bright flowers that shone in the morning light. She could just see Mazzy on it with a yellow helmet and Jack running along beside her, coaching all the way. She was so full of love she didn't think she could contain anymore.

And then the woman came back to the door cradling a little ball of calico fuzz. It mewled a couple of times and Chelsea's heart went to full burst.

"Here you go. Jack put a hold on the kitten, too, saying he had to make sure it would be good at the house. You got a beauty here. She'll do you good." She handed the cat over and it started purring. "He said he wanted the calico and he wanted a boy, but I told him that wasn't possible. Calicos are girls. I figure he's already outnumbered. Why not a she cat, too?"

Tears spilled again, and again they were happy ones. Mazzy had been asking for a kitty for six months now, but Chelsea had had to tell her no because they couldn't have a pet at their apartment, not to mention who on earth would take care of the poor thing when they weren't home.

But now they would have a different home and different circumstances. She resisted the urge to pinch herself to make sure this was all really happening.

She turned with the cat in her arms. Jack's smile split his face. "You don't have to bribe her, you know. She already likes you."

His laugh rang in the blue sky. "I'm hoping that maybe that little fluffball will keep her busy so I don't get trounced at Candyland all the time."

Chelsea carried the kitten on her lap the rest of the way to her parents' house, thinking about how life could change on a dime. Having Mazzy had turned her whole world right, Paul's leaving had turned it upside down, but with Jack's help it was now turning back around to perfect.

Mazzy was out in the front yard when they pulled up.

"Hi, Mommylove. Hi, Big Man!"

"Do you think she's going to be okay with us getting married?" Jack asked as they sat for a moment in the car waving at Mazzy.

She would not start leaking out of her eyes again. "Yes, I think she will love it. She loves you, and so do I."

"I bet you she's going to love me even more when she sees that little one." His smile was contagious.

"No more bribery after this, Jack Barton. You're going to have to be a disciplinarian, too. Molding is bigger than just giving hugs."

He turned to her, his face serious and his eyes focused only on her. "I know that, Chelsea. I'm going to do everything I can to be the best dad I can be. I do believe that I have an advantage, though, because I have you, the best mom ever, to learn from. But before we get into the serious stuff let's go have some pure fun."

"Deal."

Chelsea got out of the car with the ball of fur in her arms and a smile on her face. No matter what they faced, they would have each other. Jack was strong and so was she. Together they had always been a good team, and now they would be a partnership.

Mazzy saw the cat when Chelsea was three steps from the gate. The little girl clasped her hands to her mouth with her eyes opened wide.

"What is that?" she whispered.

"This?" Chelsea nuzzled the kitten to her cheek. "This is your new friend, if you want her."

"But we can't have kitties at our house, Mommy. I don't want to leave her here unless I get to stay, too. I don't want to go at all."

Mazzy was going to wind herself up to crying at any moment. Jack snatched her up before she could get herself to full throttle. "How about we go in and talk to your Grammylove? Your mom and I have some good news to share with you and your new kitty."

"What kind of good news?" she asked, skepticism clear in her voice and the way she looked at him. "I don't want to go back to our stinky old 'partment. That would be good news."

"Then we have the best news, baby."

"Really?" She grabbed Jack around the neck and squealed, then demanded to be let down. "Tell me, tell me. But first let me hold the kitty."

"Actually, first we're going to go inside where you can sit down to hold the kitty, and then we're going to talk with everyone."

"Okay!" And she ran into the house yelling that Big Man and Mommylove were here with her kitty.

"Are you sure you're ready for this?" she asked with the small cat purring against her chest.

"I have never been more sure of anything in my life, Chelsea. I want to make a life with you and that ball of energy that just ran into your mother's house. The inn needs a little livening up anyway."

"I hope you know what you're getting yourself into," she said, but smiled.

"How do you know it's not that *you* should be aware of what *you're* getting yourself into?" He pinched her butt and had her yelping.

"Oh, you're going to pay for that."

"That's fifth on my list of things I like to hear."

"You'll have to show me that list."

"Only if you're good. Now let's get in there and make your parents as happy as we are. This is a long time coming, Chelsea. Are you sure you want to turn this one-week thing into a lifetime?"

She reached up on tiptoe and used her free hand to pull him down to her. "I have never been more sure of myself. You are in for the ride of your life."

"Looking forward to it." The gleam in his eyes said that they'd discuss that more later, too. "We'd better get inside before I take you back to the inn and let your mom know we're going to be a few more hours."

And just in time, because Leigh Moore was out on the porch with Hugh and Mazzy, who was jumping from one foot to the other. "You have one very excited girl here, and I hear there's a kitty coming in the house. Any other news you want to share?"

"I'm engaged!"

"It's about time it was real," her dad said.

They all laughed as they went into the warmth of Chelsea's childhood home. It reminded her that Mazzy would call the inn home, and Chelsea couldn't think of a better way of fulfilling all the promises she'd made to herself and her child on the day she was born.

They were home for good.

A word about the author...

Misty Simon loves a good story and decided one day she would try her hand at it. Eventually she got it right. There's nothing better in the world than making someone laugh, and she hopes everyone at least snickers in the right places when reading her books.

She lives with her husband, daughter, and two insane dogs in Central Pennsylvania, where she is hard at work on her next novel or three.

She loves to hear from readers, so drop her a line at misty@mistysimon.com

Thank you for purchasing
this publication of The Wild Rose Press, Inc.
For other wonderful stories of romance,
please visit our on-line bookstore at
www.thewildrosepress.com.

For questions or more information
contact us at
info@thewildrosepress.com.

The Wild Rose Press, Inc.
www.thewildrosepress.com

To visit with authors of
The Wild Rose Press, Inc.
join our yahoo loop at
http://groups.yahoo.com/group/thewildrosepress/